Under a
Turquoise Sky

Under a Turquoise Sky

Stories of Three Cultures

Short Stories by
RAYMOND J. STOVICH

ENTRADA BOOKS
A Division of Northland Publishing

*I dedicate this book
to my parents,
John and Ann Stovich,
who taught me
the value of a good story.*

FIRST EDITION
ISBN 0-87358-540-2
Library of Congress Catalog Number: 91-51147
Printed in the United States of America

Cataloging-in-Publication Data
Stovich, Raymond J.
    Under a turquoise sky : stories from three cultures : short stories / by Raymond J. Stovich.
    104 p.
ISBN 0-87358-540-2 (softcover) : $9.95
    1. New Mexico--Fiction. I. Title.
PS3569.T6747U54   1992   91-51147
813'.54--dc20   CIP

Cover Design by David Jenney
Text Design by Carolyn Gibbs

"The Santero" was originally published in *The Ligourian*, February 1991. "Coyoteway" originally appeared in *Indian Life*, Jan./Feb. 1991.

The haiku found in "The Emergence," first appeared in *frogpond*, the journal of the Haiku Society of America, vol. xi, no. 2, May 1988.

4-92 / 2.5M / 0399

Contents

Acknowledgments

E ach of the stories in this book began with an encounter. Some word, phrase or glance, delivered in a moment's meeting, somehow affected my soul and passed into my memory. For some reason these moments kept working inside of me, working on me, forming questions and intimating answers. At some point imagination came to work on these memories. These stories are the work of imagination on memory.

I did not set out to write Hispanic or Native American stories. Some of these stories are, however, set in Hispanic contexts, some in Native American. This is to remain true to the context and presence of their initial encounters. From thence the dictates of my soul and the play of my imagination took over to create my own stories. All except the Coyote tales: of these what can anyone say?

I wish to thank Jerry Kilbride and Mike Riggs for their support, careful reading of each story, sometimes in multiple drafts, and always useful critiques. Additional thanks go to Ruben Mendoza who created the Spanish aphorisms found in some of these stories. Thanks to my wife Linda, who put up with the lunacy of living with someone who could find no other option than to sit in front of his word processor for hours and hours and hours.

I also want to thank Susan McDonald, Nicky Leach and the staff at Northland Publishing for having faith in these stories and for making the multiple tasks of getting them published painless and even pleasurable.

All of the stories, including "The Weaver," are works of fiction. Any resemblance to actual persons, groups or historical events is purely coincidental. I wishes to thank *Ligourian Magazine, Indian Life,* and *frogpond* for permission to reprint the material that first appeared on their pages.

The Santero

I heard no rooster, he thought, as he tried to raise himself out of bed. Maybe that no-good coyote got him. Julio García y Ortega felt the room sway. He let himself back down to the well-worn groove in his mattress. "Oh that *medicina*—it will kill me before my heart does."

The old man laid there and focused his vision on his hands. They were as bony as the roots of the cottonwood tree, the wood Julio used to carve his *bultos*, his little saints. "Either my hands are shaking or I need a new pair of eyes. No, it is my hands again."

Slowly he looked around his kitchen. Though the house had two bedrooms, Julio was living his life in just this one room. The curtains were blue calico, a little yellowed, a little dusty. Plates were neatly stacked on a shelf next to the corner fireplace. On the table were the candlesticks he had made for his wife's sixtieth birthday. In fact, except for some dust and a few stains, nothing in the room had changed since Stella died three years ago—nothing except Julio. The order helped keep his soul at peace.

Julio García y Ortega tried to will his hands to stop shaking. "How can a *santero* make statues of the *santos* when his hands are shaking like those of a drunken man?" He once again slowly raised himself and looked at the workbench on the other side of the room. "Today I must try again to make that santo of San Ysidro for Father Perez." He liked to carve this saint more than any other. He liked the story of how San Ysidro wanted to do nothing more each day than to worship *Díos*. In fact, García y Ortega was the most famous of his generation of carvers primarily because of these bultos, these carvings of Saint Isidore. Julio even left these statues unpainted—colors would only distract from the deep way they moved the heart. People called García y Ortega "The San Ysidro Santero."

"Father Perez is my friend. It was he who married me to Stella. I cannot disappoint him." With these words the old man rose and prepared himself breakfast, hoping it would leave him alert and able to carve his santo. He had been hoping to get to it for the past three weeks. Each day, though, after his morning coffee, he picked up his chisel, approached the wood so carefully dried and prepared and stared at his shaking hands. "O Díos," he would console himself, "my spirit is willing but this 74-year-old bag-of-bones is weak." Today as he held his morning coffee, Julio noticed his hands grow calm. A good sign, he thought, today will be special.

Halfway through his tortillas and coffee, Julio heard his granddaughter calling to him from the front gate. The old man looked forward to these visits. Except for an occasional tourist trying to get a good deal on a santo, hers was the only other voice heard in the old house.

Julio got to the door just as Angelina knocked. The door was never locked, but her mother told her to knock first anyway.

"My favorite little girl, what did you bring me today?"

"*Abuelo*, mama made a very good chile verde yesterday. It should be even better today. Do you want me to warm it up for you?"

At least his daughter sent him a meal each day, even if she "could no longer bear to enter that depressing place anymore," as she put it.

Julio looked at his granddaughter standing at the stove. He noticed how her jeans fit tighter and how her blouse was getting full. Julio remembered Stella when he first saw her at a fiesta. How beautiful and how ripe.

"My granddaughter Angelina, soon you will be visiting with young men and you will no longer need your old abuelo."

The young girl blushed.

"No, Grandpapa, that will not happen. I heard Mama and Papa talk yesterday. They didn't know I was listening. Mama wants you to live in our house. She told Papa that you are too old for your tools. She wants Papa to take them away from you before you hurt yourself with them. You will not hurt yourself, will you?"

The old man laughed and kept laughing until his granddaughter joined him.

"Angelina, let this be our little secret, just ours alone, okay? Now you go or you'll be late for your school bus."

Julio was troubled. He did not want to live with that bossy daughter of his. But more than that, he could not live without his tools, without his carving. *Para un santero, escultado y respirado es lo mismo.* (A santero who no longer makes santos has no right to breathe.)

Julio shut off the flame under the pot of chile and went to his workbench. His hands were shaking. O Díos, he thought, I hope that daughter of mine is not right.

Julio García y Ortega reached into his pocket and took out an old rosary. He had carved the cross and beads himself and had given it to Stella on their wedding day. She used it every day of their married life, and Julio felt close to her spirit when he used it to count his Ave Marias. *Santa María, Madre de Díos, El Señor sea con tego . . .*

Julio did not notice the door open. It was the banging that distracted him. Only then did he look up—to be blinded by the sunlight streaming into the house. Slowly he began to make out the outline of a man dressed in the black coat and felt hat of almost a hundred years ago.

"Well, can I come in?"

"Who are you, and what village do you come from?"

"*Compadre*, can I not have a chair? My feet are so tired."

Julio motioned to the visitor and kept squinting at him. Suddenly Julio's eyes opened like an owl's. He quickly made the sign of the cross over his forehead and his heart. He picked up two chisels, formed them in a cross and pointed them at the stranger.

"Relax, my friend, I am not the Devil. Quite the contrary. Old man, you should know me by now, what with all those carvings."

"San Ysidro?"

The visitor smiled.

"But how can it be? You look so real, so alive."

"Compadre, compadre. You people are all alike. And I thought *you* of all people would have more faith. Here, give me one of those chisels." The saint took a gouge from the carver's hand, picked up a piece of scrap wood from the floor and started

3

to carve it. "You think ghosts could carve wood?"

Julio shrugged, a tacit agreement with the visitor's impeccable logic.

"Is that coffee I smell, my friend? That is the one thing I miss nowdays. Mind if I pour myself a cup?"

Even before Julio could answer, Ysidro was up at the stove, pouring and sniffing, sniffing and pouring the dark brew. "If you pardon the expression, this is heavenly."

A mumbled "*Madre de Díos*" was all that Julio could muster.

"Now, now, Julio, watch your tongue. Wouldn't want to offend anybody, would you?"

"You tell me you're San Ysidro, but I cannot believe you. You don't act like a santo."

"You want me to go around like a Jesuit? Why should I? I'm happy now. I've reached my goal."

Julio got up to put on a fresh pot of coffee.

"A little chicory, too, if you have it. I miss that stuff."

In a few minutes, each with a steaming mug, the two men sat down and began to talk like friends. San y Sidro asked Ortega about his family, his health and the crops. He commiserated with the old man's arthritis and heart problems. At one time he had arthritis also. Julio asked about the Virgin, Our Brother Jesus and about Stella. He was glad to hear how happy Stella was. His heart was glad for her, but the dull pain of his loss became pointed.

San Ysidro asked Ortega to show him how he made his famous statues of the saint. Once again, as in times before, the carver forgot his miseries.

"Tell me, who is this little guy you always put next to me?"

"That is funny, *mi Patrón*, you do not recognize the angel Díos sent to plow for you?"

"Why would He do something like that?"

"But it is your legend. You were supposed to plow, but you wanted to pray, so Díos sent an angel to plow for you so you could spend the day praying."

The saint roared with laughter. "No doubt another priest made that one up. It was not like that at all. Yes, all day I would plow, and yes, some days it seemed like the plowing would never end. But God did not send an angel to do my work for me. My work became my prayer. My feet and my muscles worshiped our Father. And I learned to find Him in the smell of the dry brown earth, the heat of the sun making sweat run down my face and the breeze that cooled me off. Hmm, I wonder why we have no coffee in heaven. Anyway, compadre, there was no angel."

Julio García y Ortega thought about this. He knew what it was like to lose yourself in a task—carving was like that. Nevertheless, his face was troubled.

"If what you say is true, then all of my bultos are wrong. And if I started to carve what you told me, no one would believe me. They would say I'm too old and I lost my mind."

Now it was the saint's time to think.

"I have the answer, compadre. Keep carving those little angels. There are many people who could not understand the truth even if *I* told it to them. That story's a good one for those who want to believe it, and it is harmless for anyone else. But there is one problem."

The santero held his breath.

"The beard. Can't you see I have a beard, a big shaggy one at that? Not that tiny pointed one you always make."

Julio let out a sigh. "Just in time. See, I almost cut off too much wood for a shaggy beard. This will be the only santo of San Ysidro with such a shaggy beard."

"Oh no, my friend, you will live to make many more."

Ysidro finished another cup of coffee, made one last appraisal of his friend's handiwork, and then gave a quick nod of the head.

"Until next time, my friend. I must go."

Almost as soon as the door closed, it opened again and San Ysidro stuck his head back into the old man's house. "By the way, I wouldn't tell that daughter or son-in-law of yours about our talk." The santo shook his head and left.

Julio García y Ortega put the finishing touches on his latest bulto. There was no doubt in his mind that this piece was his best work. He was glad he had made it for Father Perez. Then the old man stretched and walked to the stove. He did not notice it was still morning, but he did notice the chile was still hot—and good and spicy.

The Storyteller

As Sonny Peña was escorted across the plaza to the tribal office, he saw Freddie DiSilva close the door and walk away with a look so smug that it made his mouth as dry as an arroyo in August. Sonny was led through the adobe that housed the tribal office. It had twelve rooms, all added on at different times, all built at slightly irregular levels.

This reminds me of the story Professor Mentes told us of the Minotaur and the labyrinth of King Minos, he thought. I hope I can find my way out.

The door to the innermost room was open. Sonny's silent escort indicated that he was to enter.

The Pueblo Council, one elder from each of the twelve kiva societies, met in this room. They sat on the floor, each of them on a red blanket, one of the signs of their office. Their braided hair glistened silver-gray. Sonny Peña also noticed Jacinto Flores, known in the pueblo as Gray Badger. Jacinto Flores was not a member of the council. Rather, he was the best known of all the Pueblo sculptors and painters. He wore hand-tooled boots and turquoise jewelry worth over a thousand dollars; his house was a new-style ranch house filled with all sorts of modern art. What saved him from criticism was the fact that he contributed almost twenty percent of his earnings to the people of the Pueblo of San Marco. In fact, Sonny's tuition at the University of New Mexico was paid for by the Pueblo Council from Gray Badger's contributions.

"Swift Clouds, we hope we have caused you no inconvenience." Johnny Red Horse was the *cacique* of the Turquoise

Clan, and therefore head of the Pueblo Council during these six months. He called Sonny by his Pueblo name and spoke in the traditional forms of the Old Language, which Sonny and his father had practiced all week.

"Swift Clouds, we thank you for coming at such short notice." Everyone in the pueblo had known about this trial for weeks.

The old man pulled some papers out of his flannel shirt and a pack of native tobacco from his Levis. He rolled a cigarette, lit it and passed it around the room. It was a sign of their oneness in spirit. Then he continued to address Swift Clouds, Sonny Peña.

"When you became a man of this pueblo you were told that telling a secret of our People is the most serious harm you could do to your brothers, uncles, fathers, grandfathers and to yourself. Your father and his father and his father before him have been at one with our People, as you have been for the years of your life. But it is said that you have revealed a secret of our People. This is very serious."

The Pueblo of San Marcos was like the other Río Grande pueblos in most respects. It was, however, the most conservative in and secretive about its ritual practices.

"Swift Clouds, you have been in the white man's school in the city, and you have spoken what you have in the white man's way of speaking, which not all of us understand. You know our brother Gray Badger here. We have asked him to sit with us because he is very much one with our People, and he knows the ways of the white man too.

"In the name of your father and his father, in the name of our People and Ancestors, speak with a pure heart."

Sonny waited for about a minute as his father had instructed him, and then he began, "My grandfathers and my fathers, I speak to you with a pure heart. As you know, my grandfather was a great story-teller. In the winter months many of you joined us in listening to his words. And my father is well known for the words he speaks."

Sonny noticed many of the men nodding in agreement.

"You know that I study in the great school of the white man, the school called the university. I study the stories of the people of many nations and especially of the people of the many nations across this great country.

"Each year at the school there is a contest. It is like the running contests we have on the days we dance our most sacred dances, only it is a contest for storytelling."

As he spoke, Sonny moved his eyes towards each of the old men, letting them fall on the floor at their feet. He watched them, though, out of the corner of his eye. This was his most important performance, and he needed to be in touch with his audience.

"For this contest at school the storytellers do not speak their words. They write their words on paper.

"This year Freddie DiSilva and I both entered the contest. Freddie DiSilva wrote about his first week at school. I wrote about how our People came up from the first three worlds into this our present world."

No one moved. No one made a sound. But Swift Clouds, Sonny Peña, felt the tension in these men's hearts and minds.

"I spoke of nothing which is not already written in the words of the men who have come to study our People, the same men you gave permission to speak what they saw and heard. I told no secrets.

"My story was chosen by the professors to win the twenty-five dollar prize."

Sonny added a few more details, explaining how he and Freddie had been rivals all their lives and how they argued after he had won the competition. He finished his defense with the traditional words "Thus and so I speak to my brothers and uncles, to my fathers and grandfathers. I speak with a pure heart."

Swift Clouds expected the silence that followed. Even though he knew these leaders of his People were deep inside themselves judging the truth of what he said, Sonny still felt his heart pounding in the middle of his throat.

One of the elders sat forward. Sonny smiled to himself at the way his *chongo*, his long braid tied with a red cloth, dangled against his pot belly.

"Little brother, I hope I do not disturb your thoughts."

"Grandfather, I would be honored to hear your words."

"I do not know the ways of the white professors, but why would they pay someone twenty-five dollars for words already spoken by someone else?"

"Grandfather, I mean no disrespect. It was because of the way I told my story. All the words in the books try to tell the story in the way a Pueblo would speak it. I was like our brother, Coyote. I told the story in the way the white men tell stories. The professors thought that was very clever. I used the money to buy more books of stories told by our brothers of different nations. This I speak with a pure heart."

Silence returned. Most of the men sat with their heads down and their eyes closed. To an outsider it might seem as if they were falling asleep, but to one familiar with the ways of San Marco, it was a sign of intense activity.

White Eagle Feathers cleared his throat and sat forward. He too was dressed in jeans and a red flannel shirt.

"Little brother, I hope I do not disturb your thoughts."

"Grandfather, I would be honored to hear your words."

"Would you speak your story to us so that we could decide for ourselves if you revealed a secret of the People?"

Sonny Peña tried to hide the pride he felt in his short story, but he was sure the old men weren't fooled. He only hoped they wouldn't hold it against him.

"Grandfather, I mean no disrespect. I have my story with me and I will speak it as you request."

Coached by his father in the art of storytelling, Sonny Peña held his story in his right hand, more for effect than from necessity, and began . . .

> My name is Julio Sandoval. At least that is my Spanish name. My Indian name is Two Bent Trees. That is the Indian name by which I am known to outsiders. But my name does not matter. What matters is that I am a survivor. In fact, I am the last of the survivors, those who came from the Lower World. Let me tell you what that was like.
>
> It is impossible to imagine what the absence of light will do to a person. I do not mean just a winter gray sky, or even a month of such relative darkness. I mean a darkness absolute and total. That was our

condition. It didn't matter if our eyes were closed or open. Our flesh grew soft and spongy. The only muscles that continued to work were those we exercised while groping, defending or feeding. But that was not the worst of it. At every breath, for there was no day or night, we breathed in the darkness. It penetrated our skin. It filled our lungs. We pumped the darkness through our hearts and minds. We became nothing more than that black darkness. Actually, black is a color you can see. For us it was more like pure nothingness.

Afraid of being trampled upon, we slept only when we collapsed. We would often feel the presence of others, sometimes hear their whimpers, but in the darkness we never identified ourselves. Make no mistake, we felt that, that pain, for we desperately wanted something or someone to fill the emptiness, especially the emptiness inside.

None of us knew then what we know now. I mean none of us realized that there was a being such as Great Father Sun. It was He who took pity on us. He created Rainbow Warrior and Lightning Man to lead us out of the First World, the World of Darkness, to the World of Light.

The pain when we first saw Rainbow Warrior and Lightning Man was immense. It was the first time our eyes really saw, and even the faint glow of light was excruciating, but even more painful was the vision we had of our desperate selves.

Sonny Peña continued to read his story, telling of the gradual emergence from one world into the next until the Original People finally settled in the Fourth World, the land upon which we now dwell under the blessing of Great Father Sun.

Things started to look real good for us the first few days in this new world. Lightning Man dried out the land so we could walk. Rainbow Warrior made it light some of the time and dark some of the time so we could both work and rest. Then one day one of our men went off to explore this world. When he crawled back, his flesh was torn in strips. He was barely able to speak. He told of a great beast covered with fur. The next day one of the women went out of camp and came back with her hand clawed off. Once again the blackness rose in our hearts. We called out to Great Father Sun.

The Protector heard our crying out and again sent his two helpers. Rainbow Warrior called together one of all the animals of this new world. They numbered the same as we did. Lightning Man sent out one of his bolts of power and turned each animal into a stone. Lightning Man and Rainbow Warrior formed us into two lines and touched each of us with a different stone. When he touched us, the power of that animal passed into us. One man became as clear-sighted as an owl at night, but he also craved to kill. Another became as hard-working as an ant, but he also wanted to banish anyone who would not work hard. And so on. Some of us took on more noble ways, some more harmful.

Soon men wanted more power. They tried to touch other animal stones. This angered Lightning Man and Rainbow Warrior.

Lightning Man shot a powerful bolt of light and shattered the animal stones into pieces. Rainbow Warrior scattered the pieces and buried them all over the land. Then they taught some people how to find these stones and how to carve them back into the shape of the animals. Rainbow Warrior and Lightning Man told them to do this whenever the People needed power. Never again would the power pass directly into the People, but they could find stones and carve them when they needed some power.

That is how man came from the World of Darkness into the World of Light.

Sonny Peña put down the papers, thus showing that he had finished his story. Everyone sat in silence. After a few minutes Johnny Red Horse thanked Swift Clouds for his true words and his pure heart. Without ceremony Sonny was escorted back to his parents' adobe.

Sonny's mother and father were eagerly waiting. Bill Peña took the lead in asking a few questions, just enough to get the whole story and the council's reactions.

"Don't worry about them taking a long time to make a decision," he said. "Even if they decided right now they will still wait 'til tomorrow to make sure it's the right one. It's just our way of doing things."

Sonny tried not to let his family see his hands shaking. Margaret Peña made her son some calming herbal tea.

Sonny really got tense when he saw the council members leaving the pueblo office. Rudy Martinez, his dad's closest friend, came by and told him that they would wait for the next day to make a decision.

Sonny was up before sunrise, but the summons didn't come until almost noon. He could feel his stomach churning all the way to the tribal office.

Johnny Red Horse began. "Swift Clouds, we thank you for your coming at such short notice. We hope we have caused you no inconvenience." He then took out the papers and the tobacco and passed around a ritual smoke. It seemed to Sonny Peña that everyone was taking a very long drag on the cigarette.

Then Johnny Red Horse shifted forward and turned towards Sonny. He did not look directly in Sonny's face as he delivered the verdict.

"Little brother, not all of us here understood the story you wrote, but Gray Badger and Fierce Bear, who went to school in the city, told us that you are a very good storyteller according to the white man's way of telling stories. Everyone agreed that you did not speak a secret of the People."

Johnny Red Horse shifted on his red carpet and changed to everyday language.

"All of us here, though, are real worried for you. It's okay to tell stories in the white man's way, but we're worried that you might get confused about what we believe here in the pueblo.

The stories might get too jumbled up and too hard to keep straight.

"You know that Gray Badger here makes a lot of carvings for the white folk. He makes good money doing that. But you know when we need power, we come to Gray Badger, and he knows how to find a stone and carve a real powerful animal for us. Gray Badger knows how to keep things straight, so we asked him to kind of sponsor you so you could learn how to keep things straight yourself. We're not telling you that you have to let him sponsor you, but we all think it's a good idea."

He sat back. There was a great and heavy silence in the room. Sonny Peña wanted to jump up and shout, but he followed his father's advice and sat for some time in silence. Then he spoke.

"Brothers, uncles, fathers and grandfathers. You are all very wise, much more than I am. I, as do all of us in the pueblo, admire Gray Badger. I would be honored to have him as my sponsor."

Sonny noticed the old men relax. The council closed its official meeting, though everyone stayed in the room for some time cracking jokes and talking with Sonny, all except for Rudy Martinez, who went to give Sonny's parents the good news.

Sonny changed a lot in the next ten years. He became an assistant professor of Comparative Literature, married, started a family, published three novels and became close friend with Jacinto Flores. Though they were a generation apart in years, and one was a sculptor while the other was a writer, both shared a passion for art. Sonny had a home in the Sandia Heights district of Albuquerque and spent most of his weekends at the pueblo. Jacinto was a frequent guest at Sonny's place. In fact, there had been only one brief, but important moment of conflict . . .

Sonny's wife had taken young Benjamin to visit his maternal grandmother, which left Sonny and Jacinto free for a day of philosophical discussion. And so, while these two friends sat on Sonny's front lawn finishing a six-pack and watching the sun set in a dust storm out in the west they got into an argument.

Their disagreement was going in circles and was getting hotter when Jacinto blurted out, "You know, for a smart kid, you're sometimes pretty dumb. Sonny, you're as bigoted as the worst of the folks back home." Jacinto immediately regretted the bluntness of his words and added, "Sorry, man, I guess I've been spending too much time in town." The apology wasn't very effective.

The issue was longstanding. It was based upon the memory of Spaniards conquering and plundering the pueblos. Not all Pueblos still carried a grudge, but San Marco had suffered most at the hands of the Spaniards and its memories went very deep.

Sonny felt the blood rise in his face. It was a good thing he had only had three beers. "Okay, wise guy," he said. "I'll bet you a punch in the gut that you can't come up with three Mexicans that deserve my respect."

"Okay, Sonny, what about that old guy we visited. The one who carves statues of saints. His work's every bit as good as a Hopi kachina. He's got a good feeling about him, too. Tries to walk a Sacred Path."

Sonny wet his index finger and drew an imaginary line on a chalk board made of air.

"Then there's that weaver just north of Santa Fe. What was her name? You said her work was better than any Navajo piece. Seems to me you said something about dating her if she weren't a Mex."

Sonny's face lost some of its radiance. He could almost feel Jacinto's fist boring into his flesh. Bravado was the defense of choice. "Okay, man, but I mean one who would actually go out of their way to help one of us. Know what I mean, *amigo*?"

Jacinto rocked on his lawn chair and took a long and slow drink. He was already savoring the victory. "You know, my friend, for a writer you sure got a poor memory. Remember a couple of months ago how Benjie was sick and that old lady down the block came through the storm to bring some herbs for the kid? Seems to me that tea she made worked pretty good. Nice old Hispanic grandmother type, wouldn't you say?"

Sonny stood up, unbuttoned his shirt and said, "Okay, so I'm just a dumb Indian. Go on, you won fair and square."

Jacinto Flores stood and stretched. A lifetime of sculpting had developed the muscles in his arms. He walked over to Sonny and smiled.

"Tell you what, my friend. I hear you're writing a book of Indian stories. Instead of me making you a cripple, how about writing one Mexican story for each Indian story. When you're done, give it to me and I'll do a few drawings."

Sonny and Jacinto sealed the bargain with a handshake, sat back and watched the lights of Albuquerque fill the night.

Coyoteway

Grandfather Tsotsie's skin was as dry as the arroyo that ran beside his hogan. He sat crosslegged on the earth and he took his time, sitting and smoking. His brown eyes smiled. Grandfather Tsotsie was going to tell me a story. He always told the best stories.

It was late one evening, in the month of *Woozch'iid*, the month of the Sound of the Baby Eagle. I was about ten years old—just like you—and I was with my grandfather tending his sheep. I respected him as a good grandson respects his elders.

I just ate my last bit of stew when I felt Grandfather's hand on my knee. Grandfather held me with his bony hand like a hawk holds a chicken. He didn't say a thing. He just held me and stared into the air. Grandfather sat quiet. He sat for as long as it takes to smoke three cigarettes, but he didn't smoke. He just sat there.

"Grandson, tell me, why does your uncle act so loco?"

I didn't know what to say. "'Cause he's sick."

"Why is he sick?"

"He gets sick when he goes to town and drinks whiskey." I was a little afraid 'cause we usually didn't talk about Uncle Set.

"Why does he drink whiskey?"

Now I really had no answer. We sat in silence.

"He drinks because he lost the *bik'e' hozoni*, the Path of Beauty. When one of The People gets off the Path of Beauty all sorts of things go bad. Like your uncle going loco."

Grandfather Tsotsie reached over and poured another cup of coffee for himself.

"So, if a man loses bik'e' hozoni, what's he got to do?"

"Get a singer?"

Grandfather nodded his head and smiled at me. Then he got up. You could hear his bones creak. He walked clockwise around the hogan to where the blanket divided it. He walked barefoot like old people walk. He walked quiet, so quiet he didn't make a sound on the dirt floor. He went behind the blanket. I could hear him fumbling with some stuff on the shelf there, some bottles and tins. He walked back, not straight to me, but again clockwise around the wall. He was carrying an old tin can. When he sat down he opened the can and took out a fat roll of rags.

Grandfather unraveled the old rags one by one. They were pictures, just like the sand paintings I saw Grandfather make on the floor of the hogans when he lead a *Naagah*, a healing sing.

"Old Hosteen Tsotsie gave these to his son, my father, who gave them to me. Your father and your uncles were not interested in them, so I saved them. They are *naskan*, memory-pictures for the Coyoteway Sing. People say when Old Hosteen Tsotsie sang the Coyoteway even the witches turned back to walk the Path of Beauty. My father sang Coyoteway and I sing Coyoteway. My grandson, I can see your heart and it tells me that you too will sing Coyoteway.

"Coyoteway is an old way. Only two of us sing it anymore. Coyoteway is an old way but it is strong. You know why it is called Coyoteway?"

I shook my head. "No."

"You watch Old Coyote, how he sometimes acts

loco. Coyoteway is for people who act loco. Them gazers and tremblers don't all know this, but Coyoteway can restore people who act loco. It can restore your uncle, but he don't let me sing it for him. Come on, we don't have much time."

Grandfather showed me the paintings and how each was changed to protect its power.

"When you paint it right," he said, "the Holy People come and live in it. The Holy People help us return to the Path of Beauty."

Then Grandfather began to teach me the songs. We sang songs of the White Coyote, the Blue Coyote, the Yellow Coyote and the Black Coyote. I thought my mind would burst. One song became another and they got all mixed up. The moon was high and my tongue would move no longer, but Grandfather gave me lots of coffee. Black, bitter coffee.

"Stay awake! Remember!" he said over and over.

Finally my brain could hold no more.

"I know you are young, my grandson, and you will forget. When it is time to remember, you go to Hosteen Big Canyon. He sings Coyoteway. Tell him I told you to come. He will teach you."

Grandfather then got up and once more walked to the shelf behind the carpet. He walked without a sound, clockwise around the hogan. Grandfather took out a bag and he walked back to me. Clockwise he walked. He handed me that bag and he said, "I went to Shiprock. That archaeologist there helped me make this. Coyoteway is the Way of your grandfather's grandfather and of my father's father. Now it is your way."

I ripped the bag open. There was a tape recorder and four tapes. I couldn't wait for my friends to see this.

"This is only for you. No one, only you, can hear this."

My jaw dropped.

Grandfather started to play the songs and show

me how they went with the sand paintings.

I must have fallen asleep, 'cause I remember Grandfather waking me up.

"Bringer of Clouds." He called me by my true name. "Bringer of Clouds," he said, "let us greet Father Sun."

We stood outside the door, sprinkled pollen and sang the *hojozi* together.

> *. . . Happily may he walk.*
> *In beauty may he walk.*
> *With beauty above him, may he walk.*
> *With beauty all around him, may he walk.*
> *With beauty it is finished.*
> *With beauty it is finished.*

After that, Grandfather turned to me and said, "My grandson, today you will do a task that is a task only for a man. When you finish you will know that you are a man."

Then he told me to run to Hosteen Begay. To run like a wild pinto. And he told me to sing while I ran. He told me to sing to the Coyote People. And he told me to tell Hosteen Begay that Grandfather is sleeping under the old cottonwood.

I started to run, and I turned back. Grandfather smiled and ruffled my hair. "No more little boy," he said, "today a man." He started to sing, "With Coyote hiding behind him . . ." and he pushed me to run.

I ran and I ran. I never looked back. I kept singing. My feet were like a drum.

"With beauty above him . . ."
I sang to the Blue Coyote People,
and to the Yellow Coyote People.
Soon I grew tired.
Hosteen Begay 's hogan was a long way from Grandfather's.

Then I heard the song in my ears and in my heart.
I heard the Coyote People singing their song.
I ran and I ran.
The song helped me run.
"With beauty all around him . . ."
"With Coyote hiding before him . . ."
I ran to the song. "With beauty all around him . . ."

My feet stumbled over rocks, and my tongue tripped on the words, but I ran and I sang.

"With beauty it is finished."

I never turned back. I never thought of anything but running. Through the wash and up the arroyo. To the White Coyote People and the Black Coyote People.

And I heard them sing too.

"With beauty it is finished."

Hosteen Begay was waiting for me in front of his hogan. Even before I could breathe, before I could tell him that Grandfather told me to run, before I could tell him that Grandfather is sleeping under the cottonwood, Hosteen Begay spoke.

"I know, my grandson. That is the way of the old people."

Hosteen Begay took me inside and gave me stew and goat's milk. I was hungry and I could not refuse the Hosteen. That would be shameful, to refuse the Hosteen's words. Then we got into his pickup, and he drove me to my mother and father's hogan. He drove fast.

Hosteen Begay never spoke much, but I remember what he said while we drove to the hogan. "Yesterday," he said, "your grandfather knew that he would finish his work here with The People. It is like that with some of the old people, they know when their path is done. Your grandfather, Hosteen Tsotsie, has become one with the trees and the earth, one with the corn and the water, the sheep and the stars. You understand, boy?"

I was just ten years old. I nodded.

"Your Grandfather walks the bik'e' hozoni in the stars. We got to take care of his old bones before sunset. That's the Navajo way. That is the Path of Beauty."

That's all the Hosteen Begay said to me. He just drove, real fast.

When we got to our hogan I ran and told my father everything that happened. I told him just like I'm telling you now.

It was the only time I ever saw a tear in my father's eye.

When Grandfather Tsotsie finished his story the hogan was silent. I wondered if he would teach me to sing Coyoteway too.

Coyote Buys a New Car
FOUR COYOTE TALES: I

This time was going to be different. Coyote had wanted a new car for a long time, but each time he went after one, some sharp salesman tried to con him. But last week a friend told Coyote the secret. "Don't seem too eager. Don't ever act like you really want the car or the salesman will rob you blind."

Coyote knew that he could act real cool, but that his tail would give him away. So this time Coyote prepared himself real good. He bought a three-pack of BVDs one size too small, put on all three and stuffed his tail into his shorts. Just to play it safe Coyote wore a tight-fitting sports jacket and over that a trench coat, even though it was the middle of July.

So Coyote went to Frontier Ford and started to hunt for a Mustang.

There it was on the showroom floor—the car of his dreams. Bright red, convertible, full of chrome and other flashy things. Just perfect for someone like Coyote. But Coyote wanted to play it real cool. He kind of walked around and whistled.

A salesman came over to Coyote as he was looking at a more conservative model. "I can tell, sir, that you have an eye for fine things. Let me show you a real beauty over here. Just look at that gorgeous red Mustang."

Coyote was trying to act cool. He didn't notice that his tail was forming a bulge under his trench coat, almost like a hunchback. The salesman did.

"Yes, sir," said the salesman, "a classy car for a classy gentleman, just like you."

Coyote was playing it cool. "Too much chrome. Too many

gadgets. Gets in the way of pure driving enjoyment."

His hunchback was beginning to quiver.

"We've gotta move this baby. New models coming in. Tell you what I'll do. You pay for just the basic car, I'll throw in all the extras for free."

Coyote's nostrils flared, his eyes grew wide and his hunchback beat with a strong fast pulse.

"I don't know. A convertible is kind of unpractical. You know what I mean?"

"I'll give it to you at factory invoice, not a penny over," said the salesman as he drew two gold-plated keys from his pocket. "You can drive it away today. It just takes twenty minutes to approve your credit. That is unless you've got something wrong with your credit rating. Well, maybe if you've got something to hide . . ."

Coyote jumped in and said, "Well, maybe I can help you out." Coyote was breathing hard as he walked back into the salesman's office.

"Let's see now. Invoice price, plus tax and license plate charges. Hey, I'll even waive the shipping and delivery costs." The salesman said nothing about the nearly two thousand dollar dealer bonus included in the invoice cost.

"Now let's see. If you want it today, we're going to have to use our fast-credit application. That's just two percent a month more, but there's no penalty for prepayment."

Just as Coyote's hunchback started to shrink, the salesman laid the two gold-plated keys on top of his desk.

"Sure," said Coyote, "sounds reasonable to me."

Coyote had to work hard to keep his saliva from dripping all over the salesman's desk.

"Then there's the points, of course."

Coyote looked vacant.

"Points. You know. Since you don't want to put up your house as collateral—you wouldn't want to put up your house for a plaything like a car—we charge you a couple of points up front. Standard operating procedure."

Coyote nodded his head.

"Now let me see, you want that little baby right now."

Coyote tried to act nonchalant, but the salesman could see the tip of his tail wagging straight up behind him.

"Of course, we have to charge you the rush prep charge. That goes straight to the mechanic."

Coyote signed the papers.

He was now the proud owner of a bright red Mustang convertible at factory invoice, with a loan at 38 percent a year, no penalty for prepayment, $800 up front in points and a $500 prep charge.

When Coyote got home, he told his wife about the great deal he got. She chased him around the block with an old broom.

The Last Missionary Journey of Padre Francisco Saldivar

Padre Francisco Saldivar lifted the heavy wood into the window opening of the thick adobe wall. His shadow flickered as the candle across the room sputtered. The priest paused to look at the flame, then lowered his gray-robed body into a dusty padre's chair. The wooden seat seemed soft to his angular old bones.

Padre Francisco tried to recite his psalms and prayers, but his mind could not focus on the words. A few years before, he would have told himself that he was too tired to pray. Now he no longer made excuses.

"Ah, *Díos*," he said aloud, "I do not know if you hear me. . ." Once again Padre Francisco watched his mind slip into what seemed liked a dark cloud.

> *It was a perfect day, filled with the bittersweet of autumn. The villagers were assembled in front of the church, waiting. Soon one of them shouted, "He is coming. The Protector of our Holy Faith. Padre Francisco is coming." The villagers made the sign of the holy cross.*
>
> *The Protector of the Faith dismounted his horse and pranced to his place at the head of the crowd. His eyes seemed to focus just above everyone's head. He spoke with the authority of God the Father. "Where is the witch?"*
>
> *Two men dragged the struggling young woman before the priest.*
>
> *Padre Francisco carefully measured his quarry. He saw her shapely ankles beneath her torn dress, her full black hair and the white marks left on her arm by*

the powerful fists of the men holding her. He saw her breasts strain as her arms were roughly held behind her. Padre Francisco felt himself come alive.

"Speak now, miserable wretch. Tell us how you enchant the young men of this village. What tricks has the Devil taught you?"

Tears streamed down the girl's face, wetting her blouse.

The sky darkened. Thunder pealed through the sky, followed by streaks of blue-white lightning. Padre Francisco summoned the forces of heaven in his condemnation.

The girl's scream pierced the heavens as Padre Francisco, with a large rock, drove nails through her hands, and pinned her to the cross where she would meet her Creator.

As he fastened her feet, a bolt of lightning crashed from the sky and struck the girl's heart. In an instant she was transformed. Hands trembling, Padre Francisco Saldivar, screamed himself awake. In his mind's eye he still saw himself nailing his Savior, Jesus, to the cross. In fact he saw a long line of crosses pointed towards heaven, each with a bloody Jesus suspended in death.

This vision was all too familiar to him, and Padre Francisco knew he would not sleep this night. He also knew his mind would find no solace in prayer.

Before dawn Padre Francisco was riding his horse on the trail to San Cristobal at El Rincón, the first mission he had established and still his favorite. El Rincón had not seen a priest since Christmas and it was now Lent, the church's time of penance and prayer. The trails were crusted with old snow.

"*Ay* Pablito, it is so good to visit during Lent, *mi amigo*." Vaqueros tending their cattle on the *llano* spoke to their horses more than their wives, and this priest was a kind of vaquero of souls, having his own four-footed companion. "Ay, my Pablito, it is so good to be with those Penitentes. What can we do but punish ourselves and repent our sins?

"I know you no longer like the cold, my friend," he tried to console Pablito, "but this time I go to save my own soul, so bear with me, my faithful friend. This will be your last journey in the cold"

Padre Francisco reached El Rincón long after nightfall of the third day of his journey and slept in the back of the church. Even before the roosters announced the dawn he had made his presence known and arranged for confessions and Mass later that morning.

The confessions seemed to begin as confession usually began—bad thoughts, bad words, a little theft and a bit of adultery—but this day Padre Francisco felt a strange and disquieting tension. "Maybe I am too tired from my trip, maybe just too old." Try as he might, though, he could not talk away his feeling.

Soon someone entered the confessional. Padre Francisco could tell it was a woman by the sound of her footsteps and the gentle fragrance of cooking herbs. He could hear her stop and make the sign of the cross. Padre Francisco was sure she was Nieves Archuleta, the wife of El Rincón's blacksmith, Fernando Archuleta.

"Forgive me, Father, I fight with my husband every night."

Father Francisco was about to say a few pious words—after all, which of these women did not fight with her husband—but something held him back. "Tell me, my daughter, what do you fight about."

Her silence made the darkness of the confessional seem more dark and very cold.

Then the priest could barely make out her shaking voice saying, "About *Tía* Eufamia."

"Well, my child, what about her."

"*Padre caro*, I cannot tell you. If my husband hears he will know I told you and he will beat me."

"My child, my dear child, you know I am bound by the Sacred Seal of Confession. I cannot tell anyone what you say."

Padre Francisco was doing his best to keep his patience with this simple woman. All he could hear were the woman's sobbing whimpers.

"Are they going to hurt her?"

"*Sí, Padre.*" Here words came out slowly and hesitantly, as if she had to make up each word as it came out of her mouth. "They think she is a *bruja*."

Padre Francisco felt the black cloud coming and fought to hold onto his mind. "Dear God," he prayed, "Even if I cannot atone for my sins, help me keep these poor fools from sinning once again."

He wanted to rush out of the church, but he held himself back. The Seal of Confession. He also did not want this poor woman beaten, and he was sure that oaf of a blacksmith would do just as the woman had feared. So he gave her penance and a blessing and sent her on her way. He sat through the rest of the confessions, only half hearing these penitents' sins.

After confessions, but before mass, Padre Francisco left the church and headed for the edge of town.

"Padre Francisco," cried out the sacristan, "Do not forget the mass."

"In a minute. In a minute." The priest was waiving his arm. "Go. Lead them in a rosary and a litany."

The sacristan shrugged his shoulders.

"Please, dear Father, do not forget the mass."

Padre Francisco was headed towards the adobe of Doña Eufamia, the old *curandera*. His thoughts were so strong that people could almost hear them.

"That stupid blacksmith, trying to accuse the old lady and stone her as a witch."

Padre Francisco thought it had to do with the blacksmith's inability to father a child, even though he kept trying with every available woman, but he kept those thoughts to himself. The Seal of Confession.

"*Buenas días, Tía Eufamia,*" he said as he knocked on the old lady's door.

"*Buenas días a Díos, Padre,*" she smiled. "If you want to meet with the Devil, you've come to the wrong place."

The priest tried to say something, but Doña Eufamia would not give him the chance. The Protector of the Faith lowered his head and bent his shoulders. He knew there was nothing he could say, but he still hoped he could help save this one person.

"Please come to mass. Let them see you take the Lord in communion."

"I am not stupid," she replied, "but I am not afraid of the blacksmith or of his lies. And I am not afraid of you for I am no longer young and attractive, and you are too old to care for such things."

In his mind's eye, Padre Francisco Saldivar, the Protector of the Faith, began to see lines of crucifixes, each with the body of Christ and the head of a young woman.

What could the priest say?

As he took his leave, the old man blessed her with the sign of the cross. He knew somebody would be snooping and would report that the old woman was signed with the cross and did not die a bruja's death.

Doña Eufamia watched the padre return to the church to begin the Holy Sacrifice of the Mass.

The words of the mass, words that Padre Francisco had said thousands of times in his life, these words formed themselves in the priest's mouth as if by their own power, and that was good because his mind had started to drift. Padre Francisco feared the visions and he used all of his might to focus on the words.

After the Gospel, Padre Francisco departed from the sermon he had prepared two nights before. He spoke eloquently and passionately of the sins of the flesh. He spoke of Lent and the need for penance. And he spoke of the human condition as despair for one's sins, a despair which identification with the suffering Christ and a long life of penance might alleviate.

Even during the most sacred time of the mass, Padre Francisco's mind began to drift. As he held up the sacred Host, Padre Francisco saw pictures. He saw an old man planting corn in the parched earth and saw a mother feeding tortillas to her hungry children. Holding the golden cup of wine, Padre Francisco saw women in labor, and children growing into adulthood. He saw the rhythms of the dark earth and the endless movement of clouds. And he saw a gray-robed missionary denying himself the touch of human kindness, denying it to others as well.

Later in the mass, just before communion, Padre Francisco's mind was filled with a vision of a blazing sun, a sun that just as suddenly as it appeared turned black and swallowed him up in its blackness.

The next thing he knew, Padre Francisco was blessing the men and women gathered at the end of the mass.

After his prayers, Padre Francisco took communion to the widow Vigil. She was dying. The priest tried to find words to comfort her, to reassure her after a long life of faithful belief, but he could not. The two old people sat in silence.

"Maybe I am losing my mind," he thought, "or maybe I have lost my faith." He shuddered at the last thought.

When Padre Francisco got up to leave he touched her forehead with a gentle kiss. The old woman's eyes filled with tears, and her lips formed a peaceful smile.

Padre Francisco mounted his horse and began the ride back to Santa Fe. "Now, my Pablito, it is time to save my soul from the clutches of the Devil." The priest chuckled and his horse snorted. "Come, let us go visit Teobaldo the Miller."

In a short time the priest arrived at the mill. He noticed that the gate moving the Río Grande's water to the large wheel was overgrown with weeds. It must have been closed for some time. The priest paused before he touched the door. For a moment he remembered this man's friendship and the many years of their estrangement.

Padre Francisco pushed open the large wooden door of the mill. One hinge was broken, so the door required a very strong push. This mill was the single two-story wooden structure in a land of earth-clinging adobes.

The priest could only see darkness, but he heard the raspy voice of the miller challenge him. "What do you want now, you old bag of fleas?" The voice came from the side of the big room used as a kitchen.

"One last time, I come to save a soul."

"I have nothing to give you, so pay a fair price for my flour and be on your way."

"For once in your life be quiet. I came to see your ugly face," replied the priest.

"So look," answered the miller. He coughed so hard that the whole building seemed to shake.

Padre Francisco did indeed look very carefully at Teobaldo Salas. Bony hands, ashen face, struggling to breathe. Padre Francisco Saldivar could practically see the Angel of Death coming to take him away.

"So you want me to die from this coughing? Make yourself useful and get some brandy."

Padre Francisco poured two full glasses, and then he said, "My friend, your hands are more white than the flour you grind."

"Yes, but I still have enough strength to beat that holy hide of yours."

"We were friends once."

"That was before you became the Great Protector of our Holy and Undefiable Faith."

"I did what I thought was right."

"And I could not stand the hypocrisy, even from an old friend."

Night darkened the mill.

"Teobaldo, I came for confession."

"Aha! I knew you wanted something from this visit. And how much for this fine indulgence? Two months wages, no doubt."

"No, my friend, not your confession. Mine."

For once in his life, Teobaldo was speechless.

The old priest got down on his knees and began, "Forgive me my friend. I have sinned against you, and myself, and all these innocent people. And I have sinned against God Himself."

The miller tried to get the priest to stop, but Father Francisco protested, "Teobaldo, I will soon die, and so will you. I cannot die without forgiveness, and there is but one person in this whole world who knows me enough to make forgiveness worthwhile. Please, if you have a bit of kindness left in your old soul, do not deny this to me."

The miller raised himself to the edge of his sick bed. The effort wracked him in spasms of coughing,

The priest continued. "Teobaldo, I no longer believe those women were witches. Twenty-three of them. I had them killed, Teobaldo, in the name of Christ and Goodness. I killed twenty-three innocent women. I deserve to burn in hell for all eternity, but I ask your forgiveness as a man."

"You old fool," said the miller. "I tried to tell you that you had

33

needs like any other man. I tried to get you to see that you only attacked the ones in their ripe flowering. But you rejected me. Too proud to see your own needs. Righteous in your narrow vision, forgetting that Jesus himself loved Magdalena. And your bishop and your Church kept you blind. You wore a skirt and condemned women. Saldivar, you do not need penance, you need love."

The priest's silence was his most eloquent plea for mercy.

"Well, I can forgive you for your stupidity. And I can forgive you for the pain you caused me, and for the precious years of lost friendship. And I can even forgive your needs as a man. But I can only pray that if there is a merciful God, He can forgive the innocent lives taken by the words of your mouth."

The sun broke over the hilltops and sparkled like a thousand flames in the waters of the Río Grande, but only a thin shaft of pale light floated into the miller's kitchen.

The priest knelt in silence.

The miller laid his hand on the old priest's shoulder.

Then Padre Francisco Saldivar stood up.

"Teobaldo, I must be on my way."

"Then go, so I can finally get some sleep."

"Let me anoint you before I go."

The miller began to laugh.

The priest pleaded, "I know of the way you give flour to the needy and make toys for all the poor children."

Teobaldo spit his reply, then showed his yellowed and cracked teeth in a wide grin.

Padre Francisco prepared to leave.

One last time, the miller spoke, "Take care of your soul, dear friend. Let us meet in the next life and make up for the lost years."

As he was shoving open the huge door, the priest turned to him and replied, "My friend, I have no fear of God. Now I know that for almost sixty years I have seen His face every time I looked into your eyes." And as he closed the old door, Padre Francisco whispered under his breath, "By now we are old friends."

Padre Francisco Saldivar saddled his horse.

"Come, Pablito," he said, "it is a long ride home."

Dancing with the Eagles

It was a long drive, the locked-up houses looked too much alike and it was getting dark. I saw an old man walk by.

"Hey, Grandfather, do you know which is María Castilla's place?"

The old man turned and looked at me. I thought he might be deaf or have cataracts or something, so I got out of the pickup and walked over to him. I offered him my hand, but he kept his thumbs hooked in the corners of his pockets. I forgot these people still don't like to shake hands. "You know where I can find María Castilla's place?"

"Who you asking?"

"I'm her son, Steve. Mom asked me to fix it up before the dances and stuff."

"You the fella the council said couldn't be here for special dances? You gotta talk to the council first."

"Don't worry, grandfather, I'm just here to fix up my mom's place."

"Second down from the Turquoise Kiva." The old man started to walk away, then he turned and said, "My 'dob' needs some work. Lots of bad rains this year. Stop by if you got time." He kept on walking.

All these old folks dressed the same way—worn jeans and a twenty-year-old Pendleton shirt—and they all walk like they have their pants full. Thanks for the help, I thought.

Then I remembered I brought up an old anthro book, *San Miguelito, City on a Mesa*, to leave for my brother Silvio. I got it out and turned to the map. Yes, that's where the Turquoise Kiva was. I had been away for a long time. Either that or I had worked hard at forgetting. Hell, what right did they have to kick me out? What right did they have to tell anyone anything?

I finally found our old house. It looked exactly the same as the dozen or so houses to the right and left of it. I unpacked what I needed for the night and got my cassette player. As I lay there trying to fall asleep I couldn't decide if I was more angry at the pueblo or at Joan. Both equally, I guessed.

In the morning, I took it easy and surveyed the place. What a mess! I was angry that Ma didn't get Sal or Jimmy to help me. It was true that I had a lot of leave coming to me, and a depressed social worker isn't very useful to his clients. But why me, and alone at that?

The sun was bright by the time I actually got started. I was sure thankful for the wind blowing across the mesa top.

The old man was there, too, sitting on a rock in the shade across the plaza. The only sign of life about him was his braided gray hair moving in the breeze.

Mixing and plastering adobe was harder than I remembered. I brought out my cassette player. A little Mozart to help set a rhythm and ignore the muscle strain. A little Mozart and a little hard work to forget about Joan. Still, not the kind of work you wanted to do in the middle of a heat wave.

I took a break and nodded to the old man. Nada. I turned up the Mozart for him to hear. Zip. I wished I had brought some Gatorade.

By five, I decided to wash up. I had finished about a third of the outside and my body already felt like I had built a three-story condo, solo.

After a can of beans, I stepped out to relieve myself. No sign of the old man. No problem sleeping that night. No old man, no dreams of Joan. I got up before sunrise to beat the heat. I hoped to go down to the lake for an afternoon swim, if the council hadn't banned me from that, too.

Once again, old eagle-eyes perched on his rock. Probably sent by the council to keep tabs on me.

Some early stiffness, but the work started to go a lot easier. A good breeze more like a gentle wind, helped, and I put on some cool jazz. Played it loud enough for the old guy to hear.

While I was cleaning up he poked me in the back.

"You want, come over later. Got some good stew."

I watched him shuffle off.

"Only about six of us live up here any more. The old women take turns cooking for me."

The mutton stew was just like Mom's, except for the extra chiles. I was glad I brought a jug of water.

"City water, huh?"

"That stuff in the cisterns is green. I can't drink that."

The old man stopped talking. Maybe I hurt his feelings. It seemed as if a vacuum sucked up every bit of sound from the mesa top. All that was left was the nighttime cold silently seeping into our bodies, cell by cell. I was relieved when the old man broke the silence.

"Couple of weeks ago, afternoon, I was having some coffee. Heard this soft rain. Real pretty kind of sound, soft like a cat's paw when he's going after a field mouse. I said, 'How come I don't hear it on my roof?' So I went to check it out. There it was. Raining between Acoma and Enchanted Mesa. You could see it coming down. Nice and real gentle."

"That's over twenty-five miles away."

Silence.

I tried to make my breathing shallow. I didn't want him to hear it.

Just then a wind came roaring up out of the plain below. It sounded like the tail of a jet about to take off, but the thick adobe walls were immovable. The wind stopped, just as suddenly as it began.

Again, the silence.

I thought I could hear the grains of dust settling back, one by one.

"Once a year they all come back. Come in their cars, music blasting. Seal off the pueblo. When they're not doing dances, they're visiting. Talking. Always talking. I think they're afraid to go to sleep. That's why they don't really know what these dances are. They talk too much. Bring the city with them. Too much noise. Can't even hear the drum beat anymore. They forgot how to listen. The drum comes from silence. That's what the dances are, too. They just forgot how to listen." Old Man Lester, as I learned his name, reached for a mug of his coffee.

Again, the silence.

That night I didn't get to sleep as fast. Not that my whole body didn't ache for sleep. I laid there and listened to the wind whipping 'round the plaza. I remembered summers growing up in the pueblo. How we would sneak around the secret path to the north cistern and make like we were Apaches attacking. I remembered the old folks telling us stories after dinner. But most of all, I remembered the dances. Not so much the corn dances, but the kachina dances. Only members of the pueblo were allowed at the kachina dances. For years I thought the men in those masks were really the spirit kachinas.

And I thought about Joan. How fascinated she was by stories of pueblo life. How she kept saying she must have been a Pueblo in a past life. I wish I had listened to the guys who said she was just out for an Indian scalp. Divorce is a funny thing when you don't see it coming. Like having someone slit your chest and rip your heart out.

Distant coyote calls, old lullabies, sent me to sleep.

Next morning I started back on the house, but this time I didn't play the cassette recorder. I finished the outside and started working on the inside walls. Lester was there, too, watching. About noon he came over.

"Got plenty of stew," he said.

We ate in silence.

"Didn't bring your kids," he said.

I shook my head, "No kids, no wife either."

Lester kept his peace.

After a while I added, "She fell in love with an archaeologist from Harvard. I guess he did more than just dig for pots."

I thought Lester would give me an Old Indian Talk, but he just shook his head. I noticed Lester used his fry bread to scoop the mutton stew, just like my grandfather did.

When I was leaving, Lester touched my shirt and said, "Got to clean the Antelope Kiva tomorrow. Getting too old to do it myself. Got time?"

I told him I was thinking of clearing out before everyone else arrived, but a few more hours wouldn't kill anyone.

Lester came to my family's place and we walked over to the South Plaza together. I wouldn't have known the kiva because it was locked and its ladder wasn't sticking out the top. Our kivas aren't round like most others. They're square, just like our homes. You gotta climb up to the roof to crawl down the ladder.

"Let me go down first, clear out the rattlers."

Lester got no arguments from me.

After I got down, Lester opened the padlocked door to the inner room. We just stood there for a while. Very little light snuck into the back storage room; mostly it just angled through the door and hit the floor. The effect was eerie, like the light of an almost-full moon in a morning sky. The old man knew the place with his eyes closed. He shuffled over to the center of the room, took a candle out of his pocket, lit it and set it in the center of the floor. I remembered this room from a dozen years ago, but even at that I was unprepared.

I saw their shapes before I saw the masks. Strange horned shapes, outlines of feathers and hook-like beaks, brooding presences from another world. Slowly the colors came into focus. A white mask with red-and-black eyes, a black-and-red mask with a yellow bull's eye where the nose should be, two horned owls, a wolf, no, it was a coyote. Their names came flooding back in childhood memories. Then my eyes let in the most frightening kachina of all. No matter how I tried to look elsewhere, my eyes came back to the center, back to staring at him. Water Serpent.

I was barely ten years old, taken from my bed in the middle of the night and brought into this room. Five of us were brought here. We were told this was the night when we would become men. We heard the drum beat and then saw Water Serpent carrying the long yucca whip. He grunted like a hungry animal. He was so tall, and his shadow covered the whole ceiling. The men holding us inched back. I was the closest, so Water Serpent turned on me first. The whip—I felt it slap against my ribs even before I heard its sound cutting the air. And then again. Another crack. Then at my knees. I almost fell over, but I knew everything depended on my standing firm. I could feel my hands shaking, and I dug my teeth into my lip to keep from crying. It was over for me almost as fast as it began, but I cringed at each smack of the whip against the ribs and knees of the other boys. Then someone lit a lantern and this great and powerful kachina took off his mask. All the men started to laugh and congratulate us. With his mask off, the kachina was only one of the men of the pueblo. That was so many years ago, the night of my finishing, my becoming a man in the pueblo. After the ceremonies we all had some cookies and soda pop and we all tried on the mask. I still feel my spine shiver whenever I look at that mask.

Lester went out to get a lantern. I poked around, running my fingers over the carved masks, over their feathers and fur. I wondered how old they were. How many generations of ancestors wore these masks, danced in them? Underground, in near-darkness . . . it was like being First People waiting in the Lower World, ready to emerge. Even though I knew these were just masks, I felt my hand tremble.

Then my eyes fell upon the eagle. Its surface was covered with carved feathers and decorated with the fuzzy down of a real eagle. Next to it hung its wings, red woolen arms with white eagle feathers attached to them. I put on the wings. As I held the mask over my head, I imagined the sound of drums and the voices of the old men singing. I started to dance. The steps quickly came back to me. I danced long strides with arms outstretched, bringing blessings down on my people. For a moment I was filled with the eagle, the clear blue sky and the earth below. For a moment I *was* Eagle carrying messages to the Spirit People, returning with their blessings.

A loud grunt brought me down. Standing in the door was Water Serpent. He was as fierce as ever, even if not as tall. This time, though, I saw no yucca whip. This time Water Serpent held a drum. I heard the drum beat and the singing of an old man. So did Eagle. Eagle danced. The steps were of the kachinas and of the ancestors, the same steady repeating steps that were danced since the People came up to this world. Eagle danced around the room. Soaring. Straining upward. Floating down in gentle circles. Eagle danced near Water Serpent, lifted his feathers in blessing. Eagle danced for a long time. Then the old man stopped singing and the drum was silent.

I took off the mask, almost in shock at what had just happened. Old Man Lester was standing there, smiling, with Water Serpent's mask in his hand. I realized that he was the one who wore that mask and whipped me during my finishing. He carried the kachina that made me a man.

We finished cleaning the place and went to Lester's for a drink one of the women made from blue corn.

I decided to wait around a day or so and talk to the council.

The Violinista

T he sound of the first bell of the day reached into the homes in San Ramón as it did almost every day of the year. But today Prudencio Vigil rang the bell louder and with more joy, for today was the feast of San Ramón Nonnatos, patron saint of the village of San Ramón. Like yeast fermenting good bread, today's excitement would begin very early and continue to rise throughout the day. But this morning, at the break of dawn, not even the most vivid imagination could prepare San Ramón for the mystery it would experience.

The festivities began with a mass in honor of San Ramón. All the old hymns were sung and Padre Estebán was inspired in his preaching of the pains of hell. As the worshipers filed out, edified and sanctified, they were greeted by a raucous little band winding its way through the dusty lanes of the village. Two musicians led the procession: San Ramón's own *violinista*, Eduardo Gómez, himself a fiddler with a very good reputation, and Hector López, San Ramón's best guitarist. They played and they sang as they marched through the town. Behind them came Don Vicente Gaspar and Don Pedro Ruíz, the sponsors of tonight's *baille*. They were followed by a growing band of village boys laughing and calling out their announcement of tonight's dance. This was *sacando el gallo*, or "calling out the rooster," the unique way that dances were announced in the villages north of Santa Fe. The troupe ended its march and played one last fast song in front of the hall at the north end of San Ramón where tonight's dance would take place.

Everyone knew that tonight would be no ordinary baille. The patron saint's feast day already made the occasion special, but Don Pedro had also arranged for the celebrated violinista Teofilo Ortiz to be the musician of honor at tonight's grand ball. After the procession, three old men, friends from childhood, Ignacio Valdez, Horatio Gómez and Pablo Vigil, first cousin to Horatio, lingered in the plaza.

"I heard that Teofilo learned how to play the violin when he was only five years old," began Ignacio.

"Yes, he learned it from his uncle," replied Pablo.

Not to be outdone, Ignatio added, "He played his first wedding solo when he was only nine years old. Can you imagine that, only nine years old."

The three old friends shook their heads in disbelief.

Mid-morning found Prudencio once again ringing the old bell, and the whole village gathered once more at the church. The crowd was silent, waiting, all eyes focused on the church door. Soon the sound of a flute was heard from within. It was a soft, ancient sound, like the sound of the breeze blowing in the aspen and piñon. It played the melody of an old *alabados*, a traditional hymn celebrating the power of San Ramón. It was answered by another flute, a deeper flute. The sound of the earth itself singing back the hymn's chorus.

Slowly and gracefully they emerged. In the lead was the cross-bearer, flanked by two men carrying candles, two boys carrying censers and six men, Brothers of the Light, dressed in white and carrying tallow candles. At the end were twelve more men, also Brothers of the Light, two flute players and the *resador* leading the hymns. In the middle of the group, high on top of a platform carried by six more Brothers of the Light, was the statue of San Ramón Nonnatos. The patron saint was starting his annual visit through his village.

This wooden statue was carved for the town by none other than the great Rafael Aragón. The *santo* was dressed in a white chasuble, draped with a blue-lined red robe. In his left hand he carried a staff with three crowns, signifying the riches and power he had forsaken in his earthly life and the Blessed Trinity to whom he had committed himself. In his right hand he held a monstrance, the sacred vessel which held the precious body of Our Lord Jesus. The saint's lips bore marks of red to remind people that when San Ramón sold himself into slavery as ransom for other slaves, he continually preached about God's love until eventually his captors shut his mouth with a padlock through the lips.

The villagers filed behind, women on the left, men on the right. Children came first, next old people, then everyone else. As San Ramón stopped before every house, the resador led a prayer of blessing and all the faithful responded. They marched along rutted lanes that passed for roads to the accompaniment of the flutes and a host of ancient hymns. Again and again, over and across the *acequia*, the ancient irrigation ditch that meandered through the fields bringing life-giving waters, San Ramón inspected each cut-off and dam and blessed the fertility of the earth. In the fields, even the cows seemed to blink their long lashes in homage to the patron saint.

Toward the back of the procession, Ignatio Valdez was overheard whispering to Juan María Vigil, owner of San Ramón's only store.

"Did you hear about how Teofilo got his first violin?" asked Ignatio.

"Some say from his uncle," replied the shopkeeper.

"No, no. You should know better."

"You're so smart, tell me."

"When Teofilo was only two years old he heard his uncle play the *violina*. He knew immediately that he wanted to play too, so he found a rusty old can and a board and made a fiddle. Only he had no strings. His family's pet cat came to him, put his head in the boy's lap and died right there. Teofilo's father made the cat's insides into fiddle strings for the boy. That's how it happened."

Vigil passed his hand in front of his face as if to chase a fly away.

"No, I know it is true." Ignatio protested so hard that his whole body shook. "My *commadre* heard it from the mouth of Teofilo's *niño*."

Juan María Vigil was impressed.

The remainder of the day was spent in preparation for the night's baille. Young *señoritas* fussed with their hair, their dresses and their makeup as their old *chaparones* kept watchful eyes as to the propriety of their outfits and their younger brothers teased them unmercifully. Outside, some of the men idled away the time in games of chance, some in games of skill. Some just polished their boots.

About an hour before sundown, Alfonso Valdez, the youngest brother of Ignatio, was talking with a few of his friends.

"It was last Lent. You remember when we met the Brothers from Arroyo Hondo for prayer over on The Hill? My second cousin was there and we stayed after prayers to talk. He is close friends with Padre Fellotón from Arroyo Hondo. The padre told my cousin that Teofilo learned how to play the violina one night from an angel sent by God Himself."

As if on cue the other men all together half-muttered a disbelieving "no?"

"It must be," said Alfonso, "the priest would not lie. That would be a sin."

They all agreed.

It was a good thing the dance would begin in only about an hour.

At 7:30, Prudencio began ringing the bell. He rang it long and loud as he did for Christmas, Easter or a wedding, for the feast of San Ramón Nonnatos was at least as important. Throughout the year, San Ramón had worked hard interceding with Jesus and His Father on behalf of the village's inhabitants. Today they would give him special thanks.

Within minutes, over a hundred people, villagers and guests, gathered in front of the church. On signal, Eduardo and Hector began to accompany the gathering while they sang San Ramón's favorite hymn. Padre Esteban appeared, flanked by Don Gaspar and Don Pedro. The priest was carrying the town's pride and joy—its hand-carved statue of San Ramón. The third procession of the day was formed, violin and guitar at the lead. San Ramón, the priest and the *patrones* were next, followed by all the rest in no particular order.

Within minutes they arrived at the north hall and San Ramón was given a special place between the violinista and the guitarist. Everyone gathered in front: young girls at their coquettish best, young men in their most *macho* outfits, old women in black, peasants next to gentry. Even the little children stood quietly, sweaty hands crushing mothers' dresses. The musicians began and everyone sang. The first song was always dedicated to San Ramón.

It was perfect except for one thing. No one had seen even the shadow of Teofilo Ortiz.

Eduardo and Hector played their hearts out. The patron saint had been good to them this year—Eduardo had a new son and Hector was able to buy a new bull—so they had a lot to be thankful for. At any other dance, the people would say how they played so well they must have been inspired. But not this evening. This evening even the flirting, which some said was the real reason the young men and women came to these dances, lacked passion. The *bastonero,* the master of ceremonies for the dance, tried his best to keep things lively. He varied the dances. He made sure the best-looking women and the best-dancing men were circulating around the dance floor. He had the musicians lead a *valse chiquiao,* a ritual game in which gallant young men composed songs to woo beautiful young ladies, a game which usually spiced things up with laughter and double entendres. But this evening everything except the notes of the musicians went flat.

Soon real trouble began. At first the men went out, one by one, to sneak a drink. Soon they were going in pairs and groups. The alcohol brought back old memories, old grudges and new grievances.

This night, Raul García was especially friendly with anyone who would offer him a drink. After one such "intermission," Raul returned to the hall to see his wife dancing with Paulo Gómez. He became furious and began to attack Paulo.

"You take my wife to bed! I'll make you a bed! I'll make you a bed in hell where you belong!"

Then came the fist fight.

It took six men to break them up.

Everyone laughed and thought the incident funny because everyone in the village, except Raul García, knew that it was really the shopkeeper Juan María Vigil who was paying late-morning visits to Señora García.

As the evening wore on, and as the men's nerves grew thinner, some of the old ladies and Padre Estebán grew more and more worried. The village depended upon the good graces of its patron saint to intercede with the Almighty. If the saint grew angry, or otherwise displeased, it could spell disaster—drought, sickness, a lack of fertility, or a dozen other maladies. And, to put it mildly, it was getting more difficult to see how this party could please anyone, much less a *santo*.

It was then that the stranger appeared. He entered the dance hall so quietly that no one noticed him. He was covered with dust and carried a package wrapped in a dusty old serape. Teofilo Ortiz walked to the statue of San Ramón, unwrapped his violina, knelt before the patron saint and offered a prayer. Silence spread through the room; it was as if a body had risen from the dead at its own wake.

Teofilo shook hands with Eduardo and Hector and took his place next to the two musicians. The first notes he played were a massive explosion of thunder signaling a cloudburst. The large wooden chandelier shook, its candles casting wild shadows on the whitewashed walls. Every third or fourth dance, the packed earth floor had to be sprinkled with water to keep its dust from choking the dancers. Polkas, *paso doubles, fandangos, espinados, inditas* and *waltzes* poured forth and brought body and soul to life. Along the walls, the old chaparones remembered how their own flirtations brought chills to their young bodies and frowns of disapproval to the faces of their own chaparones. Tonight they would look the other way. Men had visions of immense wealth and power, and women felt the stirrings of nobility in their hearts and minds.

The sun was already far along on its journey before anybody realized it. Padre Estebán lead the group in a morning Angelus and a hymn to San Ramón. Then another procession, the town's musicians leading the way, to return San Ramón to his place of honor in his home church, where he would be available whenever anyone needed his help during the coming year.

Teofilo stayed behind at the old hall. After Benediction, Don Pedro sent one of his sons to invite the musician to breakfast, but the violinista was nowhere to be found. Teofilo Ortiz seemed to have vanished into thin air.

Three days later, Ignatio Valdez was having coffee at Juan María Vigil's store.

"Yesterday I went to visit my brother at Arroyo Seco," began Ignatio. "You know, that's where the violinista comes from."

The shopkeeper poured them both another cup.

"My brother, he tells me that Teofilo's wife is very sick. He says that Teofilo never leaves her side."

"That explains why he was so late for our baille," reasoned the shopkeeper.

"You old fool," returned Ignatio, "that doesn't explain nothing. Didn't you hear me say he was at home taking care of his wife?"

"Then who played for our baille? He played so good."

Ignatio answered by opening his eyes wider than it would seem possible for any human being and by shrugging his shoulders.

Juan María Vigil stood there with his mouth hanging open, making a sign of the cross, first over his forehead and then over his entire body.

About a month later, Don Pedro was visiting his friend the *alcalde* in Santa Fe. After dinner the two men were alone in the alcalde's study, when he turned to Don Pedro and asked, "My friend, there is a rumor that you had a mysterious guest at your baille last month."

Don Pedro nodded his head.

"The peasant folk are saying that it was San Ramón himself who took on the disguise of Teofilo Ortiz and came to play for your village."

There was a long period of silence.

Then Don Pedro looked his friend straight in the eyes and whispered, "Stranger things have happened, my friend, stranger things have happened."

Coyote's Blind Date
FOUR COYOTE TALES: II

Coyote got tired of spending Saturday nights howlin' by himself, so he asked some of his friends to fix him up with a blind date.

Coyote spent all Saturday getting prepared. He paid a kid a quarter to clean his car. He washed his tail and fluffed it with a blow drier so it would be big and natural. He even went out and bought himself a white Panama hat. Coyote was going dressed to kill.

At first he couldn't find his date's apartment and started to get real mad. He thought his friends were playing some kind of joke on him, like the kind he usually played on them. Then he realized he couldn't find the place because it was on the second floor behind another apartment.

Coyote spiffed his shoes with one of those premoistened towelettes you get at the bus station. His tail was straight out and gently wagging as he rang the doorbell, but it fell flat as soon as his date opened the door. She was a dog. Now you very seldom see a coyote go out with a dog, but Coyote did his best to hide his disappointment while he secretly figured out how he could get even with his friends.

Coyote sniffed around the apartment. It was simple but tasteful. Coyote noticed lots of different smells, including more than one coyote's, so he figured that maybe he would get lucky anyway. His tail started to wag again.

Coyote took his date by the arm and led her to his pride and joy. It was a '57 Chevy. No doubt she would have preferred a fancy Mustang.

"I won't get my dress dirty in this old thing, will I?"

Coyote was very proud of his car. He held the door open for her, but he didn't bother to close it.

"Where would you like to eat?" asked Coyote, showing his pure white canines.

"Oh, anywhere," she replied, her tongue hanging out the window.

"How about Mexican food?" asked Coyote. He heard no argument, so he headed for his favorite place. Good homestyle food, lots of it and cheap.

All dinner long, his date talked about jerk coyotes she had dated. When dessert was served, she cleaned a teaspoon with her napkin and said, "This is a sure scuzzy place, isn't it?"

Coyote excused himself and went to the men's room. Once there, he squeezed through the open window, snuck around to his Chevy and drove up to the hills for a night of howling.

The Weaver

When meeting Narcissa Montoya, one is instantly embraced by the atmosphere of harmony in her home studio. Skeins of dyed wool are arranged in delicate gradations of color and texture. Baskets of roots, twigs and other sorts of materials, the basis for Ms. Montoya's natural dyes, line one of her walls. Prominently placed are her two looms: a restored antique loom and her oversized, custom-designed loom. In the midst of it all sits Narcissa Montoya, auburn hair, vibrant, petite, orchestrating this universe, it seems, with long and delicate fingers that belie the strength and dexterity acquired by years of working her loom. Narcissa's voice is soft and deep, and her words flow as sprightly as her shuttle speeds across the loom.

RAMÓN SANCHEZ: Ms. Montoya, traditional forms dating back to the early days of Spanish settlement are so important in your weavings. Do you come from a long line of weavers?

NARCISSA MONTOYA (laughing): Heavens no, Mr. Sanchez. My mother, God rest her soul, could hardly sew a stitch to save her life. But generations back weaving was a part of life. Nothing fancy. The clothes you wore. Blankets to keep you warm. So I guess in that sense weaving is in my blood.

RS: When did you first realize you wanted to be a weaver?

NM (Ms. Montoya walked over to an old *trastero* and returned with an antique blanket woven in a traditional Río Grande pattern.): This blanket

Reprinted from *Imagining New Mexico*, Vol. 7, No. 4, 1984.

has been in our family for years. It was woven by my great-great-grandmother, I think, as a present to her husband for taking care of her when she was sick. My mother and aunts tell me that when I was a child I would spend hours holding and rubbing this blanket. They would tease me, saying *"La vas a sobar a nada."* "You'll rub it to nothing." It's become a kind of family saying.

RS: That blanket planted the seeds of your later work.

NM: One day as a child I was watching my great-grandmother weave something. She was the last in our family to weave naturally. Anyway, hour after hour I watched her. I tried to summon the courage to ask her if she would teach me. At that age I was forbidden to even touch her loom. I finally asked her. I can still see her toothless smile and feel her hand on my shoulder as she said, "No, *nieta,* you are too young to be a *tejedora,* a weaver, and I am too old to teach you."

RS: You said that she wove naturally. What do you mean by that?

NM: That's simple. Today, learning seems to be hard work. We choose to be weavers. We study to learn our craft. In the old days weaving was something that was passed on without fanfare. You made tortillas, raised your children and wove your clothes. Simple. Matter-of-fact.

RS: So when did you learn to weave?

NM: When my husband Alfonso was taken to Viet Nam, his family took me in. They came from a long line of weavers. I needed to survive financially. They helped me out. And they taught me well. Very high quality stuff. Commercially made yarns and tourist designs, but high quality.

RS: How did you get from tourist designs to museum-quality originals?

NM: Well, I was tired of doing the same thing over and over, and I had saved some money. Then I got news of Al's death. The next year was horrible. Looking back I think I really went crazy. I think I could have been, maybe should have been, put in a hospital. I left the family's workshop and bought an old loom, the one you see here. But I really didn't know what I was doing. I didn't want to do tourist stuff. I knew that. But I had no idea of what else to do. So I sat. I stared at the loom and the four walls. It got real bad, but I don't want to talk about that.

RS: Yet you made it through that time.

NM: Yes, I liked to sit and watch the black spiders weave their webs. I sat on the porch and watched them. So beautiful. So graceful. Hours would go by. Then one day my mother said she heard about some sort of convention or something for traditional weavers. She offered to pay my way. It would be a birthday gift. That was the first of the Río Grande Textile Workshops at the Folk Art Museum back in '72. Looking at the weavings gave me the same feelings I had when I was a kid holding that old family blanket. I especially liked the colors. Not harsh like the commercial colors. Natural. Soft and very special. I started to experiment with natural dyes.

RS: Where did you obtain the natural dyes?

NM: From these hills, and from my neighbor's gardens. You see, you couldn't go out and buy these dyes. Especially back then. I had to learn where to find them. To pick them. People thought I had finally lost my mind. Gathering roots and bugs and things by day. Cooking them at night. Hanging them out to dry in my front yard—the place was filled with all sorts of colored leads of wool. One day my aunt came to visit when I was grinding up bugs in my *metate*. I was trying to make cochineal. The next morning she sent the parish priest to check me out— she was afraid I was possessed by the devil and made into a *bruja*, a witch.

RS: So that was the start of it all, a witch's kitchen?

NM: Well, almost. I now had the dyes and the lovely wool. But I still didn't have a clue as to what to do with them. I would sit at the loom and try this and try that. I didn't want to make the old tourist stuff, but none of the designs I came up with were any good. Then one night, I remember it was a full moon, I went outside to look at the newest spider's web and to listen to the coyotes. That's when it hit me. Spiders have been weaving the same webs for hundreds, maybe thousands, of years. Each one the same as all the others, yet each one also special and unique. Each one made for just that time and place. Then I realized what I was doing wrong. In trying to be so different I was cutting myself off from my own life and blood. That's when I realized I needed to relearn to ways of the Old Ones, the ways of the time when weaving was as important as cooking and raising children. I needed to stop racking my little brain and open up to the wisdom of my tradition.

RS: And the rest, as they say, is history.

NM: That night I got out our family blanket and started to rub it again. I traced the lines of blue—like the *acequias* that run in the spring. I could almost feel the cold water rising up my arm. I looked at the blue veins in my arm, and for a while I had trouble seeing where the blanket ended and my veins began. And I rubbed my hand on the beige. I always liked the beige because it reminded me of the walls of my grandmother's adobe. After a while I started to weave. I followed our family design—it was a blue diamond *saltillo* design on a beige background. The shuttle seemed to fly through my fingers. I caught myself singing the old songs we sang when I was just a little girl. You know, *"Naranja dulce, limón partido,"* and others like that. I worked at my loom for twelve hours straight, and I haven't stopped weaving since then.

RS: Your reputation, though, is that of an innovator and not a traditional weaver.

NM: I think that's partly due to the way I am made. I would get too bored doing the same patterns over and over, or just copying someone else's work. Also, the times are different. People have more free time. People study art. They want decorations and collections. I am part of this world too. I live in it. Each time I sit and prepare to weave, it is different and also traditional. One part old. One part new. Like this dress I'm wearing. I knitted it myself based on an old serape design. You see, combining the old with the new. I think if Al were alive that's the way he would want it too. I think he would be proud of me.

RS: Where do you go from here? What's the future hold for Narcissa Montoya?

NM: Next month I start teaching someone else how to weave. An apprentice. Really, just my niece. And I'm going to weave a lot more, I hope. I want my things to be passed along in families, like our old blanket. I hope my work will inspire other weavers.

Evening was approaching as our interview came to a close. Narcissa Montoya and I stood on her porch and watched the sun's intense light illumine the Sangre de Cristo Mountains. Ms. Montoya turned and said, "You see that sunlight? The way it shimmers? The way it plays with the shadows? How it makes everything so mysterious and alive? Someday I hope to weave like that."

Homecoming

It was Monday morning. Mondays were tough because the senior center was closed on Monday. That meant that Johnny would be on his own for lunch and dinner. But more than that it meant no one to talk to. No one to break the spell of his constant sadness. No one. Certainly not Edna. So Johnny Svensen stayed in bed.

About noon Johnny made a decision, and it gave him a reason to get up. Johnny decided it was time to visit Edna. He put on his wrinkled old clothes. He was never particularly attentive to his clothing, but before he retired, his clothes were at least cleaned and pressed. That was before Edna's cancer. That was before she had left him.

Now Johnny knew it was time to visit Edna. Maybe it was even time to shave his six-day-old stubble. But then again, why go through all that trouble?

As Johnny stepped out the door he almost fainted. The dark, cool inside of his old adobe had left his lungs unprepared for the 102 degree heat, and his eyes, clouded with cataracts, could feel only pain. It took him almost fifteen minutes to steady himself, but it was time to visit Edna.

Johnny took the long way to the bus stop. He wanted to stop at Grebhardt's Hardware. It would be easier to stop there than spend who knew how long digging around the tool shed.

"Johnny, you old coot. Haven't seen you in ages."

"Nothing much to buy. Why should I waste my time in here? Say, where you keeping the laundry line these days?"

"It's about time, Johnny," said Bob Grebhardt, wrinkling his nose.

"You don't want my money, I can go to that Sears Roebuck."

"Now don't get so testy. I'll always give my old friends top-notch service, even if I have to fumigate the place afterwards."

Johnny Svensen bought fifty feet of heavy-ply cotton rope and a linoleum-cutting tool. He walked out the door with as sprightly a step as he could summon. In fact, for the first time since Edna's cancer, Johnny felt good, felt like there was finally going to be an end, now that he was going to visit Edna.

Johnny waited for the bus a long time. Dark ovals grew under his arms, and the other passengers waited upwind. Johnny didn't notice. It was not that Johnny's mind was drifting. In fact, today, Johnny's mind was so focused that he would have missed the bus had it not been for the pesky noise those kids made.

Johnny hated the noise, but he was glad that he saw the bus in enough time to get off the bench and shuffle to the door. In fact, the only thing that mattered was that he was going to see Edna. He flashed his senior pass at the driver, who wrinkled her nose. People looked the other way as he ambled to an empty seat.

The kids in the back were already cutting up. Johnny clenched his bag a little tighter.

Don't worry, he told himself, not much longer.

He let his mind drift. It took him to familiar places. It took him to the grove of cottonwood trees where he and Edna used to go. Edna liked the grove, especially on late afternoons when the wind came in off the mesa.

"Hear that, Johnny," she would say, "sounds just like Kokopelli playing his flute." Edna loved the old Indian stories, and she was especially fond of Kokopelli, the humpbacked flute player who carried the seeds of all life in his hump. Johnny never heard Kokopelli, he just liked to be with Edna. More than anything he loved to be with Edna, silent under those trees.

Johnny let his mind drift. It was like watching a moving picture show of the different times he and Edna spent under those cottonwoods. His mind came to one afternoon, much like this one with its so very hot sunlight, when he had enraged her.

"You know, Edna," he said to her, "this cottonwood would be the perfect place to die. Hell, when I go you could just string me up and let the birds and the desert finish me off."

She wouldn't talk to him for the rest of the day.

Johnny liked the silence, though.

Johnny roused himself from his daydream and clutched the bag. "We'll see about Kokopelli," he whispered loudly enough for people to turn their heads. But Johnny didn't notice.

In fact, Johnny Svensen could hardly believe his eyes, much less pay attention to the old busy bodies on the bus.

Right there, right at the next bus stop, Edna got on the bus!

Johnny knew that his mind was likely to play tricks on him at his age. The doctor warned him not to go out when the temperature got over 100 degrees. But here was Edna and she walked right up to his seat, sat beside him and turned to him.

"Jonathan Svensen, you sure are a mess." (Only Edna called him Jonathan, and only when she was mad at him.) "Haven't you washed your clothes even once since I went into that hospital? If you don't care about yourself at least don't embarrass me."

Johnny was speechless. He quickly hid his bag under the seat.

"Well, don't you have anything to say?"

"Wh. . . when did you get out?"

"Why, Johnny, I don't know what you're talking about."

"The hospital. The cancer."

"Johnny, you know I was just there for a few days. And that stuff they put in me, well, it took away all the pain. And you were such a sweetheart. But look at yourself now."

Johnny tried to speak but he couldn't bring out the words. He opened the collar of his work shirt and tried to take in as much air as he could.

Finally words came out. "I was just coming to see you." Johnny kicked the paper bag against the side of the bus.

The kids got off the bus at the Winrock Center.

Johnny and Edna talked about old times. About how they met, Johnny the baggage master of the Albuquerque Station and Edna a Fred Harvey girl. They talked about their first date, and their special picnics at the hot springs out on the Jemez.

Johnny never noticed the stares of his fellow passengers.

Johnny and Edna talked about the cottonwoods and about Kokopelli.

"Let's go back there right now," she said.

The bus was nearing its last stop, and the grove of cottonwoods, now part of a neighborhood park, was only a few blocks away.

In his rush to get off the bus, Johnny almost forgot his package. The driver seemed impatient as Johnny went back to look for it.

"What's that?" asked Edna.

Johnny seemed not to hear.

"Jonathan, I asked you what's in that package."

"For me to know, for you to find out."

Edna laughed and they strolled hand in hand, oblivious to the stares of the passers-by.

It was early evening, but it was still as hot as midday. Even the cottonwoods offered no respite.

Johnny and Edna sat under the trees as they did in the old days. Soon the wind blew in from the mesa.

"Listen, John, it's Kokopelli. Just like the good old days."

Johnny Svensen still could hear only the wind soughing through the leaves, just like the old days. But he liked the sound of the wind. And he liked being with Edna.

Soon Johnny opened his bag, measured out the rope and cut it with the linoleum cutter.

Edna was perfectly still, staring at him.

The leaves seemed to hiss in the wind.

Jonathan Svensen formed the rope into tight curls, just as he had practiced in his mind, and made the knot tight.

Edna remained still.

A gust played through the leaves.

"I was coming to see you, Edna."

Jonathan tested the rope as he spoke.

"I was coming to see you."

He threw one end of the rope over a branch of a cottonwood. It rustled the leaves.

Edna remained silent.

Johnny adjusted the rope.

"You know, Edna, I never could hear Kokopelli play that old flute of his."

Edna held the loose end of the rope and welcomed Johnny home.

Eulogio Martinez

O h my bones," Eulogio Martinez mumbled to himself, "we gonna have some storm." The *viejo,* the oldest man in the village, made a small sign of the cross over his forehead and his heart as he tried to find a position that would allow him some sleep. Early next morning, on his way to see if his favorite hen had left him breakfast, Eulogio glanced at the mountains. He did this each morning, but today as he stared hard at the Truchas Peaks, he shook his head and again made a sign of the cross.

For the rest of the village of Santa Cruz de las Montañas, today seemed no different than any other August day. The men went to their fields, and the women worked around their adobes. An occasional glance at the Truchas Peaks meant nothing. Late summer storms went as fast as they came. Usually.

By midday, the men were back from their fields and the women were serving beans and tortillas. Though the sun was little more than a hazy gray spot in an even more gray sky, the day was very hot. Even the chickens kept to the shade.

Filadelfio Delores and his wife Macrina decided to have their meal out under an old cottonwood in front of their adobe. For the children it would be a picnic. For the adults, the wide open space would make the noise less irritating. There was nothing unusual about the meal.

"Mamá," cried Estrellita, "Ricardo keeps putting ants in my beans."

Estebán and Honorio got into a fight.

And halfway through the meal little Eugenio blurted out,

"Mamá, look at the clouds. They are like eggs when you get them so big and fluffy, only they are *so* black."

Filadelfio glanced at the clouds and back to his wife Macrina. They said nothing.

After eating, Filadelfio went about the low-lying fields, gathering his sheep and cattle. He noticed the other men of Santa Cruz doing the same, herding their livestock up to higher ground. August storms came and went. Usually. But no one forgot the storm of fifteen years ago, and the flooded river, *acequia,* fields and homes. Everyone remembered, but no one spoke of it.

As the sun moved on, the clouds seemed to get bigger and bigger, and blacker and blacker. Some of the women made *taquitos* with their leftover beans and offered them to their *santos*, the pictures and statues of the saints displayed in every house in the village. Some just lit candles. Eulogio Martinez, the viejo, decided to go to the church.

"San Francisco," he said as he placed some *frijoles* at the saint's statue, "I know you cannot stop this storm from coming, but please take care of those *animalitos.*"

"*Santo Niño,*" he prayed to the statue of the Holy Infant, "you brought food to the prisoners, and saved many ships at sea, keep us safe."

His prayers finished, Eulogio Martinez felt tired, so he lowered himself against one of the side walls of the church and, before he knew it, was sound asleep.

Outside, over and over, from cloud to cloud, lightning flashed white and blue, making the clouds appear even more black. The echo of one thunderclap crashed into new thunder and fell from the sky right onto the village of Santa Cruz. Soon the river was overflowing the little dams that channeled its waters into the network of acequias that crisscrossed the valley.

Filadelfio and Macrina came from good people. Not wealthy people, but good people. They owned land at the end of the acequia, at the low point of the valley. Most of the time Filadelfio worried that his field would dry up.

As Macrina was lighting another candle and soothing the fears of their children, it entered Filadelfio's mind to check on his fields. When he saw his chiles under water, a sick feeling took over his stomach. He rushed back inside.

"Macrina, *arriba*! Take what you want and let's go to the church."

"But what should I take, and what about our chiles?"

Filadelfio could see the panic tightening Macrina's face, but he was too afraid to comfort her. "Take what you and the little ones can carry. I'm going for the bull and the cow." As he was going out the door he added, "God can have the chiles."

The lightning was now coming so fast that it lit the path for Macrina and her children. When she got to the church, María did not notice Eulogio, who was still asleep.

In the darkness of the next hours, small groups of pilgrims made their way to the church, seeking both high ground and the Hand of God. Family by family, they entered the building that their fathers and grandfathers had made with their own hands. The *burros,* sheep and cows huddled in the back. Young children clung to their mother's skirts on the left side of the church, and the older boys took their places next to the men on the right side. Each new family brought a wave of whispers—news, tears and supplications.

"I saw a whole cottonwood going down the river, roots and all," said Porfirio Díaz.

"We heard a sheep in the river, but by the time we got there we could see nothing," said the Vigils.

"The mother ditch, she is overflowed, all the fields are gone." When they heard Sebastiano's news, everyone made the sign of the cross over themselves and their children.

"Filadelfio, your adobe. I'm sorry, my friend." Marcellino Cruz added to the news. "You can sleep with us as long as you need."

The Members of the Brotherhood of the Light, commonly called the Penitentes, grouped together to begin formal prayers. Santa Cruz only had a priest once a year, so the officers of this group of men protected and guided the faith of the village. The men had brought the statue of *Nuestro Padre Jesús* from the *morada,* the private chapel of the Penitentes. This statue was a piously carved life-size figure of Jesus at the moment of his humiliation. It was normally only carried out on Good Friday, the day of Jesus's passion and death, but today was a special day of passion for Santa Cruz de las Montañas.

The lines in each person's face were made deeper by the lit candles they held. Tonight no one would complain about the hot wax dripping onto their hand.

The *resador* began a litany of supplication.

"Heart of Jesus . . ."

The thunder answered.

"Blessed Wounds of Our Savior . . ."

More thunder.

"By Your Crown of Thorns . . ."

A deafening boom filled the church. In the silence that followed the villagers whispered, "Have mercy on us."

More candles were lit.

Then the old hymns, the *alabados,* were sung.

Afterwards, the resador told the story of Noah and the flood, and how *Díos* promised never to destroy the earth by flood again.

Juan Santiago Vigil and his family entered the church. Their adobe was the highest one, built next to the church. They entered, soaked, out of breath.

All of the inhabitants of Santa Cruz de las Montañas looked at their spouses and children in silence. Someone began a hymn. Instantly, with one voice, all joined in and sang as fervently and loudly as they could, hoping their voice would be loud enough to reach God's throne in spite of the deafening thunder.

It was during this alabados that Eulogio Martinez was awakened by a man calling him by name.

"Eulogio, viejo."

The old man looked around but all the men were filled with the alabados.

"Eulogio, viejo."

He heard it again, and as he looked up he saw the statue of Nuestro Padre Jesús beckoning to him. He opened his eyes wide. He asked himself, Why would the Master call to me? Eulogio returned to the hymn.

"*Arriba, viejo!*" This time the voice was stern.

The old man made sure his white shirt was buttoned and adjusted his dusty black suit coat.

The others thought Eulogio was going to light a candle or something. Besides, who would openly criticize the viejo.

As Eulogio approached the statue, he felt his whole body shaking.

"Come, take my hand," Jesus smiled at him.

Eulogio fell to his knees, weeping, kissing his Master's left hand.

The rest of the villagers continued to sing their hymn, but the tempo was a bit slower and the volume a little softer.

"Viejo, take my hand," Jesus repeated.

Eulogio was confused.

He reached for the statue's right hand, but as he let go of the left hand, one of Jesus' fingers broke off.

Eulogio screamed.

The blood drained out of his face and hands.

The villagers saw what happened.

Some murmured. One man cursed. They all made the sign of the cross over themselves and their children.

Lightning hit a tree nearby.

The thunder was instant and deafening.

Eulogio screamed, "Díos, have mercy," and ran to the door of the church. He was holding the finger of Jesus.

Eulogio Martinez pushed open the church door and ran into the torrential rain. In seconds, he was waist-deep in water.

"Díos, have mercy," he screamed, as he threw himself into the water. "Díos, have mercy," he cried.

Strong hands grabbed the frail old man and pulled him to safety, but the finger of Nuestro Padre Jesús was gone. Eulogio had dropped it into the raging waters. It would never be found.

In their shock and in their fear no one noticed that the thunder had stopped, and soon after, the rain.

It was not until late the next evening that the waters were back within their banks, and it took days for the land to dry again. Penitente brotherhoods from all over Northern New Mexico donated adobe bricks and muscle power to rebuild the village.

Eulogio Martinez's home was the first to be rebuilt.

Doctor Coyote
FOUR COYOTE TALES: III

As Coyote approached the front door of St. Mary's Hospital he slipped on his long white lab coat. Hunting just wasn't as good in the city as it was in the country or on the farms. The only sheep he could find were in supermarkets, and there everyone expected you to pay for what you took. But here at the hospital—things were different.

"Mornin' doc," said the bony-faced cop at the side entrance.

Dr. Coyote just growled.

On his way to the cafeteria, where doctors got free hamburgers, two baggy-eyed interns cornered him for a consultation. "Doctor, could you give us a hand with these photos?"

Coyote loved to look at x-rays. All those bones. All those luscious inner organs.

The three doctors stepped into a viewing room. One of the interns placed an x-ray against a light board and flipped the switch. Coyote's eyes grew wide, and his stomach growled. The x-ray was of a young woman's thigh, but for Coyote it was a vision of a magnificent leg of lamb. Coyote's tail grew fat and bushy. He let out a deep, throaty sigh, "Boy, what a femur."

The interns squinted at the black-and-white film.

Coyote moved away from the puddle of drool forming at his feet. With one hand he was holding his tail down under his coat.

"Doctor, that's marvelous. Just look at those hairline fractures. No wonder she's in pain. Great eyes, sir. Thanks again."

The young interns raced out, eager, no doubt, to get their hands into some casting plaster. Coyote was eager to get his teeth into some hamburger.

But . . . just as he was making it out the door, another intern stopped him. Coyote wondered where all those interns came from and why they kept consulting with a hungry, greedy Coyote.

This one displayed an x-ray of someone's liver. Coyote licked his lips, his eyes grew wide. "Hmmm, tender."

The intern replied, "No, sir, I palpitated it myself. No tenderness. But what do you think about his kidney?"

Coyote replied, "I like liver better than kidney."

The intern was considering Coyote's words when Coyote let out a growl. "I want more pictures. You know, different angles. Maybe one of those magnetic scans."

"Yes, sir. I'll order them right away."

Coyote was finally free. He rushed to the cafeteria before any more of those kids playing at being doctors could get hold of him.

"Hiya, doc," called Gladys the grill lady. "Your usual? Two burgers, rare, coming up."

Coyote pulled in his tongue and nodded his head.

Reckoning

*B*reathless. Legs cramping. His mind telling his body, "Keep moving. Keep moving."

Hearing them gain ground.

Tito dared not look back. Seconds were too precious. He had often seen them. Seen their defaced bodies, deranged minds.

Tito tried to find a new path.

Down a short alley, around a corner, through a park.

He knew their eyes were damaged, that they pursued by smell. Tito searched for water to throw their senses off. He ran through a park looking for a fountain, anything.

He was on new ground, unfamiliar.

Tito tripped. He cursed under his breath. Not too loud. Didn't want them to hear.

As he got up, there they were. Right before him.

Tito ran towards the bleachers of an old stadium. As he ducked under, he practically ran into the blinding light. It was a blast, like a nuclear explosion . . .

Next he was sinking in a kind of quicksand. It was red—blood red. He was sinking in bloody quicksand. He looked around. There were thousands like him. Hundreds of thousands. The bloody sand oozed up his chest, up his neck. His mind told him not to struggle, but his body ignored his mind—and the bloody ooze dragged him lower. Two more centimeters to his lips.

Dr. Tito Vinzoni jerked awake, screaming. Before his conscious mind was fully aware, his hands were reaching for the plastic oxygen mask and the valve at the top of the green tank next to his bed. Tito Vinzoni no longer needed conscious attention to give himself oxygen. This dream had awakened him so many times in the past three years that getting oxygen was as routine as an air raid drill. Dr. Vinzoni needed it to be this way. There was no one he could depend upon to give him his precious breath. He lived alone.

Tito Vinzoni, one of the principle scientists involved in developing America's first atomic bomb, bought The Ranch shortly after July 16, 1945, the "Day of Trinity." He wanted a country getaway, and having it so close to the site of his greatest triumph was an added bonus. In the old days scientists and statesmen were part of a steady stream of visitors, most attracted by Vinzoni's good spirits. As the years went on, however, Vinzoni grew morose, seeming to take personal responsibility for each atomic test and every nuclear accident. Soon even his old colleagues attending tests at the nearby White Sands Missile Range stopped visiting this self-made outcast. Nowadays he had only one visitor.

The dream, really the nightmare, always left him unable to return to sleep. Tito had dreamt a similar dream most of his adult life, that is ever since he saw pictures of the results of his handiwork, Hiroshima and Nagasaki. He couldn't quite remember when the dream first came. At first, only once or twice a year. At some time it became a monthly apparition. It was only since his own diagnosis of cancer that the dream came almost nightly. He prayed that it would come late in the night, giving him at least a few hours of sleep.

Tito Vinzoni looked at the clock on his bedstand. Its red digital numbers looked like the readouts on a control panel. For a moment he could not tell if the seconds were moving forward or counting down. Two-thirty-eight-eighteen . . . tonight he would have hours of predawn time.

Tito Vinzoni reached for his computer. It was mounted on a special tray that rolled over his bed. He laughed to himself, "I'm so shriveled. If this thing ever fell on me I'd be crushed to death. That would show them—computers *are* hazardous to your health."

In truth, Vinzoni loved to sit in front of the monitor's pale green light. It chased away the darkness. It comforted him. It kept the brooding at bay—until daylight came.

Rosie Martinez found the old man sound asleep, his hand resting on the computer's keyboard, his thumb on the "period." On the screen Rosie saw lines of periods endlessly following each other in a crude imitation of infinity.

"Wake up, professor," she said, as she gently shook his hand, "time for your bath."

Tito was glad to see Rosie, his visiting nurse. He tried to tell himself that he was glad because Rosie's being there meant that the night and its inevitable terrors were over, and that a fresh supply of peace-inducing morphine had made its way to his house. He tried, but he feared that he was getting quite dependent on this genial woman.

Rosie pushed aside the computer and adjusted the flow of oxygen in his plastic mask.

Tito grumbled and pushed it away.

Rosie began the bathing ritual.

As she was washing him, Tito Vinzoni held his arm next to Rosie's. Her dark, thick arm made his baggy skin seem almost transparent, as if his bones showed through.

"You could use me to teach anatomy," he said, as she rolled him to one side to change the sheets.

"Tough night again, professor?"

"Don't turn psychologist on me."

"How'd you know I was puttin' myself through school?" Rosie was indeed studying to be a counselor.

A few seconds later she blurted out, "It's okay to be afraid of dying."

She felt his body stiffen and his hand withdraw. Immediately she blushed and regretted her boldness. "I'm sorry," she tried to correct her mistake, "it's none of my business."

Silence filled the room.

As she came close to the end of her task, Rosie spoke, "I guess it can be pretty tough. You need more morphine?"

Vinzoni grew irritated. "You don't understand. I'm not afraid of dying. It's my life I can't live with."

Rosie wiped her face with a towel she kept dangling out of the back pocket of her jeans. "People'd give their eye teeth for your life. Famous scientist. Look here, pictures of yourself with all sorts of important people. You helped make history."

"Look at the world, Rosie. Look at the history I helped make happen."

"Well, you helped get my uncle back home alive. He was a marine, you know."

"I think we were all foolish enough to think that's what we were doing. Talked ourselves into it. Use the power just once to end the war. But you know, I think somewhere inside I knew better. Really. I just got drunk on the whole scene. That's it—just a big high. Not booze. Power. The power to reshape the world, even if we did have to destroy it as we went along. That's how smart I am, Rosie."

"Is there anything you can do about it?"

"You know I can't even get up to empty my bladder. What can I do now?"

Rosie's silence seemed to restate her question.

She refilled the morphine dispenser attached to Tito Vinzoni's IV and prepared to leave. "*Hasta luego*, professor. Maybe you could get some sleep this afternoon. See you tomorrow."

Tito Vinzoni waved goodbye. The cancer hurt when he moved too much, but it was the only way he could pay thanks to Rosie Gutierrez. His mind, though, was elsewhere. Dr. Tito Vinzoni, nuclear scientist and maker of hydrogen bombs, was occupied with the challenge presented him by Mrs. Rosalinda Gutierrez, mother of six and visiting nurse.

At some point he fell asleep. Somewhere, in some part of his mind or body, he felt a restful recharging sleep course through his being.

Then they came again, the gang of irradiated avengers. With them the chase, the shortness of breath, the futile attempt at escape, the explosion and the sea of bloody quicksand.

Vinzoni clutched at the oxygen. His panic was made more intense by the realization that this was the first time these avengers came during the day. His hands were shaking as he reached for his computer.

"Damn," he thought, "Rosie set it too far away."

Vinzoni wanted that screen. At the moment he had awakened from the dream, a light flashed in his brain. Every cell of his being was once again filled with a sense of mission.

Tito Vinzoni forced himself down his bed. Each inch, each centimeter brought new pain, but he needed to reach the screen.

He was at the end of his oxygen line. He ripped off the plastic mask and stretched farther—and fell out of bed. Blinding pain racked his whole body.

Tito Vinzoni was driven. His nurse and friend had challenged him. He had the answer, but he needed to reach his computer. Vinzoni would rewrite his will, making his estate a hospital and research center specializing in healing the effects of the terrible bomb he had helped to create.

As he reached for the keyboard, Dr. Tito Vinzoni saw a great light, like the explosion of a hundred-megaton bomb, he estimated. Its mushroom cloud grew larger and larger, turning in on itself. Its infolding resembled the convolutions of the human brain. The great light, turning in on itself, taking on the shape of a monstrous human brain. It was a bomb, just as he had helped to create, exploding in his head.

The Emergence

Y ou mean you haven't written a word since she died?"

Jonathan Demmings answered his son by looking out the window. Jonathan Demmings, twice Pulitzer Prize–winning author of fourteen books of poetry, essays and criticism, whose typewriter was mute since his wife died in an auto accident nearly ten months ago.

"For chrissake, no wonder. The house smells like a bar. You look like a bum. When you gonna quit feeling sorry for yourself?"

"You gonna preach, let's just turn 'round home. Shows me how much you loved your mother."

"Damn it, Dad," replied his nearly middle-aged son, "I loved her almost as much as you did. But you didn't kill her, even if you were at the wheel. Nothing you coulda done to stop that drunk from hitting you. Now we're all getting sick and tired of watching you kill yourself."

Once again Jonathan looked out the window. Jonathan regretted his agreeing to accompany Biff to Chaco Canyon for three days.

In the silence the two men listened to bugs hitting the car's windshield.

Biff glanced at his father now and then. At first all he saw was an overweight old man in a dirty red Pendleton. This man was so unlike the Jonathan Demmings that Biff knew—literate, fastidious, with a Machiavellian sense of humor. It took time for Biff to begin actually to see his father, to see the new creases in his face, the lines of grief, the brokenness in the old man's shoulders, the painful way he tried to use the brake pedal each time he spotted an oncoming car.

They had turned north onto Highway 44 when Biff looked at his father again. "All I gotta say is that Mom loved you for your poetry, and if you really loved her you would be writing your heart out instead of drinking it away."

"Is this the Salvation Army or a painting trip to Chaco Canyon?"

Jonathan lowered his hat over his eyes, reclined the seat and acted as if he were going to take a nap. Biff turned on the car's radio.

The first day at Chaco was fairly uneventful. Biff worked on his sketches, rough drafts of illustrations for a book of short stories. Jonathan killed time walking around the ruins. Between the A.D. 900s and A.D. 1100s, it is thought that the forty-three square miles of Chaco Canyon may have been filled with anywhere from two to five thousand people living in large complexes. The people eventually moved away, but their structures remained.

Jonathan was especially fascinated by the ruins of Chetro Ketl— the remains of a D-shaped building that would take up almost two blocks of a city like Chicago. Jonathan picked up a conversation with Navajos working on a restoration project.

"This sun could bake a brownie," he said as he offered the two Indians beer from his cooler.

"You know that stuff's not allowed here," replied the younger of the two, reaching for a bottle.

"Funny thing, how these people disappeared," said the older one. "Seemed to disappear into thin air almost overnight."

"Nothing funny about that," said Jonathan in a tone that jolted all three. "Sorry," he added, "I just lost my wife real sudden. I guess I still haven't gotten over it."

The diggers sat in silence, but it was a comfortable, understanding silence.

Jonathan's voice broke the silence. "I wonder if these people liked poetry?"

The Navajos were silent, the older man staring at Jonathan and fingering the red ribbon in his braid. In time he spoke, "They were Pueblos, you know. Probably put their poetry into songs."

Jonathan nodded. He liked the way these men reacted—they didn't. It was as if poetry were just a part of life. Jonathan felt a close brotherhood with these two laborers.

After a while, the workers went back to their digging. The old man turned to Jonathan and said, "I think the real good stuff was in their dances. Over there in the great kiva."

One soul had spoken to another.

That evening Jonathan sat next to a piñon fire, letting its incense conjure memories from a past most recently locked shut. He looked at the stars and picked out Orion's belt, traveling back to the first time he and Lisa had gone camping. Real camping—tents and all—not the traveling motor-home type of tourism that now passed for camping. The truth of the matter, he admitted to himself, was that Lisa never did like to rough it. She was city-born through and through. He glanced at his son seated at the table of the rented RV, transforming his sketches into watercolors, listening to rock music coming so loud from the tiny headset that Jonathan could hear it twenty feet away. He chuckled, thinking there must've been a mistake at the hospital, and again grew quiet when he admitted the truth of how much Biff was like his mother.

Early the next morning, Jonathan had Biff drop him off across the canyon at the ruins called Casa Rinconada. Jonathan picked up a park brochure as he walked the short path to the ruins. He wondered at the fact that Lisa and he had lived in New Mexico for almost two decades and had never visited Chaco Canyon, the hub of an ancient empire.

Casa Rinconada was a free-standing great kiva, a political and religious center. Each summer solstice, the people of the Chacoan Empire gathered in the great kiva for an important religious ceremony, a reenactment of the story of their origin.

Jonathan entered the back of the ruins. According to the park brochure, these were storage and changing rooms. Jonathan walked down the long underground "secret passage" that lead from the support rooms and opened into a hole in the floor of the main room. Jonathan was not prepared for the immensity, the beauty or the silence of the ruin. As Jonathan entered the round chamber, the sun rising over the canyon walls almost blinded him. He walked across the massive circle and sat in the shade on the ledge that ran around the inside of the kiva wall. In an effort to steady himself, he reached for his copy of Frazier's *The People of Chaco.*

He read that the Chacoans, like Pueblo people today, believed they were created in an earlier world, one which was geographically as well as spiritually on a lower level. With the help of higher powers, these people ascended into this current world, the Fourth World of creation. This was called "The Emergence." Each ceremonial house of the Pueblos has a hole in the floor, the *sipapu,* which represents the original hole through which the people first entered this world. The solstice ritual at the Grand Kiva celebrated The Emergence on a scale never since duplicated. By means of the "secret passage," people actually emerged from the *sipapu* of the great kiva. With costume, music and chanting the Chaco People reenacted the story of their origin.

Jonathan grew tired of reading. He returned the book to his backpack, took out a bottle of beer and leaned back, feeling the cool earth beneath him.

In the sun's glare, Jonathan thought he saw someone emerging from the sipapu. Just a park ranger, he thought, but no ranger appeared. Poet's imagination, he concluded.

The figure reentered the kiva. He was short; his dark skin gave high contrast to the white kirtle and multicolored feathers he was wearing. He walked in silence with great dignity, barely touching the ground.

Two more figures emerged, both men, both dressed identically to the first. Then two more. The men walked in a procession. The silence in which they walked added power to their ritual movement.

At the end of the line, a young boy dressed in kirtle but no feathers carried a basket. Behind him came a woman dressed in flowing white, radiating a light as powerful as the sun. It hurt Jonathan's eyes to look at her.

The procession marched around the kiva in a clockwise direction three times. At last, it approached a stone altar set in the south quarter of the kiva. Two men removed an object from the boy's basket and placed it on the altar. It was a heart carved from stone. The woman held another stone, large and heavy. Everyone turned to the altar. Their breathing was still. They were waiting for the exact moment of the solstice.

Suddenly a shaft of light entered the center window of the kiva and focused itself directly upon the stone heart on the altar. The woman raised the stone she was bearing and brought it down onto the stone heart. The stones' crash filled the kiva, echoing against its walls.

The stone heart shattered. In its place was left a living, beating human heart. At that very moment Jonathan looked into the woman's face and saw his wife Lisa.

Jonathan fell back against the wall and began to sob. His vision was over. All that was left was a memory, many memories. Jonathan Demmings began to remember. His grief came deep from the heart and his sobs from somewhere even deeper inside. The almost perfect acoustics of the great kiva magnified the sounds into a huge chorus of sobbing. It was as if the ghostly presence of the people of Chaco was helping Jonathan Demmings finally say goodbye to his wife.

After a while, a breeze began to blow across the kiva, Jonathan's mourning was finished for now. As he left, words came to him. Words! For the first time in months a poem began to form in Jonathan's head.

> sunlight
> creeping to its mark
> the ceremonies begin

And then again.

> open doorway,
> empty room—
> the silence

As he turned back for one last look, more words came.

> abandoned kiva
> old rattlesnake skin

Soon the words were coming faster than Jonathan could write them. They felt good. Like a return from the grave. Like an Emergence.

At first, Jonathan thought they were mere sketches, word

sketches that would later become poems. But that evening, sitting at the piñon fire, Jonathan realized that these jottings were not sketches at all, but full-blown poems, a kind of haiku, a strong and alive North American haiku.

Jonathan Demmings' next collection caused quite a stir in poetry's established circles. Jonathan began the book with a sequence of poems dedicated to Lisa. He called it "Chaco Canyon."

CHACO CANYON
—for Lisa Demmings

digging the earth—
looking for traces
of their farming

far wall petroglyph
a lizard

open doorway
empty room—
the silence

abandoned kiva
old rattlesnake skin

park ranger
explaining kiva rituals—
a gust of wind

a whisper
from across the ruin

sunlight
creeping to its mark
the ceremonies begin

after pictures and poems
the silence.

Mr. Coyote, Permanent Acting Chief Coordinator

FOUR COYOTE TALES: IV

As I got near, I could hear him chewing out one of his staff. Hell, you could hear Coyote howlin' down the corridor.

"I told you time and time again, 'Never take a bribe.' Didn't I tell you, 'Never take a bribe in your office?' And didn't I tell you over and over again, 'When you take a bribe, don't ever, ever give a receipt?' You dumb fool, you're gonna wreck it for everybody in this office. Now get out of my sight—take the rest of the day off."

I wasn't sure this would be the best time for a surprise visit, but I went ahead anyway. Well, Coyote couldn't have been more friendly. We sat there and chewed some fat for hours.

"Say, man, how did you get this cushy job anyway?"

Coyote howled with laughter.

Just then the phone rang. I couldn't believe my ears.

"No, ma'am, Mr. Coyote is in a very important meeting. I'll have him call you as soon as he is available." Coyote was answering his own phone with a woman's voice.

As he hung up he growled, "Damn people. Pay some taxes so they think you're supposed to work for them. What do they think the government's for, anyway?"

"So, how did you get this job?"

"Ah, it was all politics. I would go around the graveyards and get the names of the guys who just died, then I'd go and vote on their behalf. Always voted Democratic. So I got this job. But this is really a dumb job and I got to work so hard. I got to sit in this office at least five hours a day."

"Pretty tough, man. How do you keep it together?"

Coyote smiled and reached for a flask.

"Don't you ever get in trouble?" I asked.

"Not if you know the system," he said as he passed me the flask. "When you don't know something you say, 'I'll look into that.' If they catch you, swear at your clerk. And most anytime just say, 'I'll get right on it.' Most days the most I do is monitor the media for a gauge of public opinion—you know, I watch Phil and Oprah and those other talk shows."

Coyote grew real quiet and serious. I wondered if he were feeling pangs of conscience or something about the fact that he never really worked. The room was absolutely still. Coyote looked at me with those deep yellow eyes and said, "You know, working for the government and playing tennis are a lot alike. You got to have good service."

Then he winked and added, "Service is what you do to get the ball bouncing from one guy to another. Anyway, tomorrow is my last day. Going to retire, gold watch and all."

Three months later, I heard that the government rehired Coyote as a consultant and paid him three times what he got before. Now he doesn't even have to sit in his office for five hours a day.

La Bruja

The lines in the old woman's face were made deeper and darker by the firelight from the kiva fireplace of her adobe home. She was skinning an apple with a large carving knife, and as she moved her arms, the shadows above looked like a raven flapping its wings.

"Do your parents know you are here?" asked Doña Placida de la Mora.

Across the table the adolescent Diego Tafoya shook his head no. His eyes remained fixed on her carving knife. "They would not approve."

She eyed his smooth skin, its dark tan deepened by the fire-light. *Perhaps it is time for you to become a man,* she thought, *we shall soon see.*

"You must help me, grandmother. I must have María for my wife."

"So talk to her, dear child. Have your father talk to hers. Give her family some chickens and a *burro.*"

"She will not even speak to me." He lowered his eyes and slowly looked around the room, his gaze passing over all sorts of odd-shaped jars and containers. Finally, his eyes ended their pilgrimage at the old woman's face. "You give people lots of herbs and things. Please give me something so that she will desire me." He used a very courteous form of speech.

The crone's eyes flared as she jabbed her knife into the pine table. "I am not a *bruja,* a witch. I use nature's gifts to restore people and to heal them. I am a *curandera.* I cast no spells."

Diego swallowed hard and barely whispered, "I just want her to notice me for a while."

The old woman threw the remains of her apple at her scruffy dog. "*Un coyote hanriado hasta un pollo venedada se come*," she sneered, "A hungry coyote will eat a poisoned chicken."

Diego did not understand. He continued his pleading until Doña Placida de la Mora took pity on him.

"You want help from a bruja? I will send you to a bruja! I will send you to Truchas to Doña Esperanza Sebastiana. She lives in an old adobe at the far end of town. You will know it when you arrive. But first let me tell you what happened there before you were born."

The fire dimmed, and less and less of Doña Placida's face was visible.

Don Pedro Ruíz was the *alcalde* of Santa Fe, but he owned a beautiful *hacienda* in Truchas. When you go to visit Doña Esperanza Sebastiana you will pass what is left of his hacienda. At that time, the hacienda had a courtyard that was always filled with flowers. It had *portales* on all four sides so you could walk in the shade, even in the afternoon. The hacienda had a grand *sala* for dances and parties, and a *capilla,* a chapel, dedicated to Nuestra Señora de Dolores. When he was in town, the priest would stay at Don Pedro's hacienda and say mass there just for Don Pedro's family.

One day it happened that the alcalde's wife wanted new furniture, so Don Pedro hired a local *carpintero,* Diego Pantoval, to build this furniture and to remake his *portales* in the more ornate style popular in Santa Fe at that time.

Don Pedro and his two sons stayed in Santa Fe most of the time, but he kept his wife and three daughters in his hacienda. His youngest daughter was named María, and María was very bored in Truchas. Maria wanted to live in Santa Fe where there were always lots of young men who wanted to court her.

That is why her father kept her in Truchas. She spent much of her time walking in the portales, the same portales Diego Pantoval was repairing for Don Pedro.

Each day, María passed the carpintero again and again as she walked the portales, but she never seemed to notice him. Diego, on the other hand, lived for these moments. For him, the rustle of her skirt was a chorus of archangels. He glanced at her, but only briefly, as if to compare the shape of her lips or the outline of her brow with the picture of her that he had painted in his mind.

"But how could a carpintero even think that the daughter of Don Pedro Ruíz would bother to look at him?" Diego's brother asked a good question. It was no accident that his brother was the smart one.

But the answer came to Diego on Pentecost Sunday, the day the Church celebrated the descent of the Holy Ghost and the inspiration of the apostles. While Diego Pantoval was at mass, he heard the padre warn the faithful about going to a bruja.

"Would you pay a witch to get revenge for a stolen chicken and burn in hell for all eternity? Is your immortal soul worth the price of a burro?"

"Of course," thought Diego, "a bruja! And since I am not seeking revenge it will be all right with Our Lord."

In those, days every village had at least one bruja, and Truchas was no exception. Doña Esperanza Sebastiana lived in an adobe very near the far edge of the village, next to a bunch of old and gnarled cottonwoods. Few people crossed her weed-filled yard, and those who did made the sign of the cross on their foreheads while peering over their shoulders. Visitors were shocked to learn how much Doña Esperanza Sebastiana knew of them. It was said that she turned herself into an owl at night and spied on the villagers.

And so it happened the following evening that Diego Pantoval, still smelling of sweat and pine shavings, paid his respects to Doña Esperanza Sebastiana.

"You are silly with love, are you not? That snooty little daughter of the great man?"

Diego shuffled his feet and moved his hat in his hands as if he were fingering a rosary.

"So you lust after her and come to the old witch for a potion."

"Oh no, Doña Esperanza, it is not lust. I love her with all my heart and want her for my wife."

"I see. Not for lust but for a personal servant."

"You do not under. . ."

She cut him off before Diego could finish the word. "I do not care for your reasons. What have you brought Doña Esperanza?"

"I have very little. I am a poor carpintero, but a good one. I can make you a new *trastero* or some new chairs."

The bruja stared at him. "I do not need a carpintero, you fool. Do you not know that I can summon the forces of hell to make me chairs?"

Diego shuffled his feet closer to the door. Peals of laughter rang from the bruja's lips.

"You fool. Like all these villagers, you believe that priest. Doña Esperanza is in league with the Devil. No one talk to Doña Esperanza. Doña Esperanza is unclean. Until one of you needs revenge or is sick— with greed or lust. Then you hold your hat in your hands and plead with Doña Esperanza."

Diego lowered his head and moved his hat down beside his thigh.

The witch studied Diego carefully. He had good strong hands, was fairly handsome and was not fat. "Are you willing to pay my price? I do not need a carpintero, but I need a *man*."

Diego turned crimson.

The old woman did not wait for an answer but turned to her trastero, her ancient cabinet, and began to combine herbs and other ingredients, which she kept in old and unlabeled pots.

Diego stuttered his words, "But I cannot do as you ask. I am a virgin, and I wish to save myself for my María."

Doña Esperanza Sebastiana did not turn away from her work, but she sneered, "Silly boy, you think I do not know of that girl you took into the hay field last summer? Doña Esperanza knows everything."

Diego himself had forgotten about Isabella. That had been youthful lust, but this love for María was pure. And besides, he had already confessed that to the priest and had done his penance.

"Get your beautiful one a silver necklace, but first paint it with a tea made from these herbs. But be careful, my silly one, whoever wears it will burn with desire. Now take this and get out of my sight before I eat you."

Diego counted ninety-two days before he had enough money to go to a trader and buy María a necklace. He chose a silver-and-turquoise necklace, a new pattern made by Navajo silversmiths called "squash blossom." He could see the turquoise reflecting María's blue eyes.

Diego decided to give his gift to María the next Friday morning so she could wear it to mass the following Sunday. On Wednesday, he carefully brewed the tea and soaked the necklace. He did not leave it in the tea very long; he didn't want to be totally unfair. "The bruja will make María see me, but she must fall in love with me from her own heart." Thursday night was spent polishing and repolishing the necklace. Then it was Friday.

María was resplendent that morning. A new dress her mother had made for her set off her neckline and the fullness of her figure. She almost walked by the carpintero without hearing his apology.

"Pardon me, Señorita María, I do not mean to be offensive. Please—I saw this and I wanted you to have it. I bought this for you."

Sunlight reflected off the silver and caught María's

eye. "Oh how beautiful," she said as she greedily snatched it from Diego's hands. She then continued her stroll through the covered portico.

Diego regretted that he had not left it longer in the tea.

That evening, Don Pedro came to the hacienda with some guests from Santa Fe. María wore the necklace to dinner.

"A new plaything? Who is the admirer this time?" María's father loved to tease her about her seemingly endless train of suitors.

"No Papa, it is from one of the workers. I don't know why he gave it to me, but it is beautiful. You must thank him for it."

Dinner began with a chicken soup filled with chiles. Halfway through the soup María began to feel warm. Soon her forehead was soaking with perspiration.

"Too many chiles," teased her brother.

"I told you to be careful of the sun," chided her mother.

María smiled and apologized, but her fever grew. Within seconds she gasped for water and clutched at her neck. Before anyone could move, María lay on the floor. She was dead.

The priest came to Truchas to lead the wake and to offer mass for the soul of this young flower.

Diego could not believe what had happened. Tears flowed down his cheeks and choked his soul.

A few days later, Don Pedro Ruíz came to Diego Pantoval where he was building a new corral. "You gave this to my daughter before the angels took her to heaven. Here. It is yours."

That night, Diego hid a large knife under his shirt, took the necklace and once again went to pay his respects to Doña Esperanza Sebastiana.

"Blame me, you fool. I offer to help you at no cost and now you want to attack me."

"But it is your necklace. She died because you killed her with the herbs you put on this necklace."

"You simple-minded fool," she hissed. "How could those herbs kill her. Did you die when you made the tea? Or when you wiped it off the necklace? Or when you polished it or carried it to your sweetheart? How silly you are. Take this foolish necklace. I need it not." Doña Esperanza Sebastiana threw the necklace back at Diego.

Diego drew his knife and advanced on the old witch.

"See for yourself, silly fool. Put that necklace on your own neck." Her extended hand and the look in her eyes forced Diego to obey.

Within moments he felt his cheeks flush and his head go dizzy. In front of him was the beautiful María. He ached for her and she beckoned to him. "My love, my only love. I have saved myself for you. Come, take me."

At the moment of his happiness, Diego Pantoval was pierced by a sharp pain.

The next day, his naked body was found under an abandoned owl's nest just outside the village of Chama, about two days ride from Truchas. His chest was split open and his heart was carved out.

Doña Placida de la Mora reached for another apple and slowly peeled its skin.

Diego Tafoya sat perfectly still, listening to the hiss of the last ember in the fireplace.

Doña Placida de la Mora added, "Some say that Doña Esperanza who now lives in Truchas, is the granddaughter of Doña Esperanza Sebastiana. Others say she is the same person."

The room was totally dark. Diego Tafoya could no longer see Doña Placida's face. In the silence, Diego Tafoya heard an owl hoot.

Under a Turquoise Sky

T he Tumbleweed was typical of the east side of town. Pink concrete adobe, a neon cactus with a tumbleweed that lit up in three places to simulate motion—these were its classy points. Some nights the dust was so thick the locals joked it poured out of the beer spigot. Dori Serrano was a Wednesday-night regular at The Tumbleweed. She liked it because no one knew her and no one asked questions.

Dori always sat at the far end of the bar. She liked to watch Julio's wife and kids through the door to their back room apartment. They looked like a happy family.

Then there was Derek. His deep tan made his blond hair shine, and his blue eyes looked like the sky. And he didn't have the pot belly that was the stock-in-trade of most of these construction workers. Dori had begun to like Derek. She was ready to break two of her rules. Rule Number Eleven: Don't date guys from The Tumbleweed, and Rule Number Twelve: Keep the Tumbleweed and Real Life separate.

Dori Serrano was the only nurse employed by Bernalillo County who spoke both the Pueblo languages of Tewa and Keresan. Consequently, she was called whenever a Pueblo Indian was brought to the BCMC in bad shape—mostly old people with chronic stuff gone wild, some tiny infants who needed emergency care to survive the next twenty-four hours, and the usual victims of high-speed accidents. So Wednesday nights at The Tumbleweed were her sanctuary, and now she was tempted to blow her cover.

Dori's entrance had become something of a ritual. "Hello

beautiful, *cómo 'stas?*" from Julio, followed by whistles and cat-calls from some other regulars, finished with Dori's, "I'm not Norm, and this place doesn't look or smell like Cheers."

Dori Serrano took her usual seat and did a quick scan of the room. She noticed that Derek had not yet arrived. It was already a quarter past nine. Through the open door way she watched Julio's wife trying to put the kids to bed.

A few beers later, Dori was watching Bill Eisenhood doing the weather on Channel 4 when she felt someone grab her waist. Instantly she reacted with her best self-defense training. Her scream got everyone's attention. Derek was gasping for breath, more embarrassed than hurt. Dori was blushing.

"That was the most stupid thing . . ."

"I was just trying to be friendly. How did I know you was a female Rambo?"

"Well, don't be friendly with my body. Got that?"

Derek sat with his friends that evening. Both of them drank too much, and Derek was still going at it when Dori left.

The stairwell was dark, and Dori fumbled for her keys. She nearly tripped over a box as she entered her apartment. She made it to the sofa and was out for the rest of the night.

She woke early. Even a hangover couldn't break that habit. A quick gargle, a tall o.j. with extra sugar and a long shower. Dori washed her hair three times, and she scrubbed her skin twice. Afterward she opened the windows and put her Wednesday-night clothes into a plastic bag that she placed inside another plastic bag. No one had invented a detergent strong enough to eliminate the smoky smells of The Tumbleweed. But it was more than that. Rule Number Twelve: Keep The Tumbleweed and Real Life separate. Once again, that might be easy to do.

Dori decided she didn't want to spend her day off alone in her apartment, so she went to Old Town, had lunch at Christopher's and sat in the plaza reading and watching the tourists.

I don't know what was on my mind last night. Dori mentally reviewed the scene with Derek. Must have been all those stories of muggings in the news lately.

Her thoughts drifted to the rest of her life. In the almost fifteen years since she had left the pueblo and home, Dori had gotten a degree and a good-paying job. Each day she worked hard at helping people and keeping her staff's morale as high as possible. Dori Serrano was respected and liked. So why did she keep going to the grungy old bar? And why didn't she have any close friends in town? Dori didn't like these questions, so she put them out of her mind by concentrating on her latest romance novel.

Later, she had dinner at a Garduno's Restaurant near her apartment, rented a couple of video cassettes and headed for home. As she settled in with a big bowl of popcorn, Dori remembered the box she tripped over the night before. She picked it up and carried it into the kitchen. Its address, scribbled in her grandmother's handwriting, was covered by a neatly printed label, no doubt prepared by the post office clerk. Dori carefully placed the package on her dinette and went to the counter for a knife.

Inside the carton was another box with a letter taped to it. The letter had her name printed on it. Dori opened and read it.

> *My dearest granddaughter,*
>
> *You know how much you are my favorite grandchild. I write in Spanish because I know you can read Spanish. I cannot write Spanish good, but at least you can read. I know you must go away from our pueblo. You are very smart and your spirit needs to travel. But you are a Pueblo. And you are of the Pueblo Earth. You must touch the Pueblo Earth or you will not be who you are. I make this pot for you. I make it from the clay like we always pick together. When I make this pot for you I pray to the clay. I say, "Clay, you be a good pot for my granddaughter." I say, "Pot, wherever my granddaughter goes you go with her. You be Pueblo Earth for her." I say to the pot, "Pot, you take care of my granddaughter." I make this pot just for you, Quick Eyes.*
>
> *— CORN GROWS TALL*

Dori was embarrassed by the crude handwriting, the misspellings and the clumsy grammar, but she carefully folded the letter and placed it in its envelope. She lifted the inner box and slowly pulled the tape.

Dori held the pot in both her hands. It was black and its polish was as perfect as only Corn Grows Tall could do. As Dori turned the pot in her hands she thought she saw her grandmother, but realized it was only her own reflection. Tears came to her eyes.

After an hour that seemed more like three days, Dori once again picked up the pot her grandmother made for her. The perfectly made black bowl had a bear paw carved on the outside—her grandmother had made a carved bear paw something of a trademark. And in the bear paw she had set a beautifully polished piece of turquoise.

As Dori held the pot it seemed as if Corn Grows Tall were with her. Dori looked at the turquoise. She was drawn into it, into the memory of the secret place near St. Clara where she helped her grandmother pick the clay she used as slip for her pots.

"Grandmother, it is so hot and you already have two buckets of clay. Let's have lunch."

They would sit under the blue sky and eat. Then her grandmother would tell Dori a story. Again and again Dori asked for the story of how her people came to their homeland. She particularly liked that part about the bear.

> . . . *so our people settled there and were happy for many seasons. But then the weather changed. The sun grew hotter, and no rains came. The kiva priests said it was because the people were not in harmony. The corn and squash did not grow. The people were running out of food, and they didn't have much to drink. Nothing was growing.*
>
> *Then one day two young men decided to help out. They decided to go out looking for food. But then they saw this big bear. Real close by they saw him."* At this point grandmother would growl and Dori would act afraid.
>
> *So these two young men tried to kill that bear, to bring him back for food, but that old bear was too smart*

*for them. He waited until the two young men were real
tired and only them did he come up to them.*

'My friends, why are you trying to kill me?'

*'We don't want to hurt you. We just want to kill you
because we are hungry and we need something to eat.'*

*'Well you don't have to kill me to eat. There's a lot
of stuff you can just pick up and eat.'*

*'But we're too thirsty to pick things up. The sun is
so hot and it hasn't rained for a long time.'*

*'Well, if you promise not to kill me I'll show you
where you can find all the water you need.'*

*They followed that bear for three whole days. At
night the coyotes would sing them to sleep. All along
the way the bear showed them how to gather different
kinds of living plants to eat.*

*On the fourth day he brought them to a land next to a
river and a lake. The young men promised to honor the
bear all their days."*

After the story, her grandmother sprinkled a cornmeal offering to
Mother Earth and little Dori helped her pick a few more buckets
of clay.

Dori Serrano carefully put the black pot into its box. She went
to sleep early that night, the first night in years that she remembered dreaming.

Dori dreamed that she was sitting in her grandmother's pot-
making room, learning from her grandmother. Corn Grows Tall
offered wisdom gained from a lifetime of work as she coached
Dori through each step of the process.

Dori Serrano was trying to shape her clay into a tall thin vase,
but she kept ending up with a lump of formless clay.

"Pots are like people, my dearest grandchild. You have to
have love in your heart or they will not come out right. Some
pots want to be one kind of pot no matter what you want them
to be. You have to love them and let them be the kind of pot
they want to be. Sure, you talk about it with them, but if you
don't love them and help them be the best they can be, all you'll
ever end up with is a lump of clay."

Dori struggled with the finishing—the sanding and polishing.

"Nothing's perfect," said Corn Grows Tall, "no pot, no person. That's why you work hard to get it to look right." Indeed it was hard for Dori, but her grandmother's patience carried her through the ordeal.

"When you bake them, you gotta have lots of hope. Sometimes they just pop in that fire. You hear that 'pop' and you get that funny feeling in your stomach, like if a close friend died or something. But that's okay. 'Cause you just grind it up and mix it with your clay for a new pot. And that one will be more strong and beautiful."

Dori hoped her pot would fire well. But instead she heard a loud "pop." It was loud enough to wake her from her dream. At first she felt sad that she lost her pot, but gradually she noticed a different feeling. For the first time in almost ten years Dori didn't feel empty inside.

The next morning Dori broke another of her rules and took her first "sick day" since she had started at BCMC. She rented a four-wheel-drive jeep, bought a bag of cornmeal and drove out in search of her grandmother's secret clay-picking spot.

Dori drove around for over an hour. Damn, it should be right here, she thought.

The sun was getting hot.

"Where are those three bunches of piñon? What if someone cut them for firewood?" she muttered.

She drove faster.

"Don't cry now. You'll find that place," she told herself out loud.

The dust cloud behind her jeep got bigger and bigger.

Dori struck out on foot. After a while, she could no longer tell if she were going in a straight line or in circles. Hot and tired, she sat to rest.

Once again she noticed the blueness of the sky.

"Like grandmother's turquoise."

She smiled as she saw the piñons.

Dori retraced her steps to the jeep. She took out the cornmeal, an old shovel and two buckets. In no time the buckets were full, and Dori was once again sitting there resting. Dori Quick Eyes looked at her hands stained with the rich clay and remembered her grandmother's words.

"You are of the Pueblo Earth and you must touch the Pueblo Earth or you will not be who you are."